Inlaid Pearl

By Stacie G. Vesolich

Xulon PRESS

Inlaid Pearl
by Stacie G. Vesolich

Printed in the United States of America

ISBN 1-597810-66-5
Library of Congress Number: 1-220-284

www.xulonpress.com

Author's Note

As long as I can remember, my family loved to sit around the dining room table sharing fond memories of Mama and Tate Moisoff. The colorful stories enchanted me, since by this time, I knew Mama and Tate (Macedonian for father and pronounced *tuh teh*) only as a quiet, elderly couple whom I called *Baba* and *Dedo*, grandmother and grandfather. Their life stories unfolded a living history of the struggles and the ultimate achievements of those hardy European immigrants so eager to secure a better life for their posterity.

As I delved into the research, particularly my grandmother's history, remote Balkan villages came to life, villages where war and destruction ran rampant and faith, courage, fortitude, and perseverance were chiseled into the human character.

Through the personal recollections of family members, years of research of the Balkans, and the diaries of my mother, Libby Moisoff George Fill, I was able to unveil a piece of my grandmother's past, as well as my mother's past and in this unveiling, a living narrative emerged.

This book is a tribute to the many brave sojourners who caught a glimpse of the future and tightly hung on to that portal, not for their own benefit, but for those who followed.

I thank my husband Steve and children Stephanie, Stephen, and Joshua (and granddaughter Alexa), for their love and encouragement to me in this endeavor. Special thanks to the Moisoff family members who willingly shared their own recollections for this book, thus creating a literary family heirloom.

Finally, and most importantly, *Soli Deo Gloria* (To God, alone, be glory), for He holds the beginning and ending of this story and all stories in the palm of His hand.

Special note: When referring to the nationality of the family, the Macedonian heritage will be used interchangeably with the terms Balkan and Slavic. Macedonia is one of the Balkan countries located in Eastern Europe. Because of the Slavic language used by Macedonians, it is also part of the broader group of Europeans known as Slavs or Slavic people. While many Eastern European nations label themselves as Slavic, nationalities that embrace a similar Slavic language are Macedonians, Serbians, Croatians, and Bulgarians.

Contents

Prologue	Baking Spinach and Cheese Pies	xi
Chapter 1	Escaping the Killing Fields	17
Chapter 2	Surviving A Boat Ride	25
Chapter 3	Painting A Family Portrait	39
Chapter 4	Ordering Donuts	43
Chapter 5	Speaking the Language	47
Chapter 6	Jumping in Corn Fields	53
Chapter 7	Surviving Infamous Days	61
Chapter 8	Buying A Store	65
Chapter 9	Playing Tambura	73
Chapter 10	Finding and Losing Love	77
Chapter 11	Raising A Princess	89
Chapter 12	Building A Home	97
Chapter 13	Living the Single Life	107
Chapter 14	Taking Care of Others	117
Chapter 15	Whetting the Musical Appetite	123
Chapter 16	Marrying Again	131
Chapter 17	Swimming and Sinking	137
Chapter 18	Having A Baby	143

Chapter 19   Healing and Recovering...............149

Rising of the Next Generation: Part II.............159

Chapter 20   Crossing Borders..........................161
Chapter 21   Taming the Gypsy Spirit 173
Chapter 22   Playing in the Band......................179
Chapter 23   Finding A New Route 191
Chapter 24   Going to College 201
Chapter 25   Going to Camp.............................209
Chapter 26   Finding A Love of My Own 215
Chapter 27   Getting Married............................221
Chapter 28   Teaching School............................229
Chapter 29   Raising A Family 235
Chapter 30   Developing Musicians..................241
Chapter 31   Singing A New Song 245
Chapter 32   Reconciling Old and New Inlaid
                Pearl 251
Epilogue   Gathering of the Clan...................257

Dedicated to my mother
Libby Moisoff George Fill

Prologue...
Baking Spinach & Cheese Pies

It was the Saturday before Easter as I stood in the middle of my kitchen anxiously glancing at the seemingly endless piles of food items scattered on wooden trays, counter tops and tables, patiently waiting their turn for preparation for our Easter meal. The abrupt ringing of the phone jolted me from my thoughts and brought a momentary pause to my culinary activities.

"Hey, Mom! How ya doing?" bellowed a voice that always brought a smile to my face. It was my son Stephen on his way home from college for Easter break. He asked a rhetorical question:

"Anything to eat? I'll be home soon, but I didn't have dinner at school before I left." I could hear the chuckle in his voice as I responded, "Stephen, now you know that there's always something to eat at home."

Three generations of family members, friends,

and local college students who lived too far to travel home for Easter, would be here on Sunday for church service followed by the usual, sumptuous Easter dinner. The household was in a state of preparation. I quickly responded to Stephen's request for food by popping a meatloaf into the oven.

As the meatloaf baked, I returned to my task of preparing a recipe handed down from generation to generation: spinach and cheese pies, called *zelnic* in Macedonian and *spanikopita* in Greek. I scanned the list of ingredients that I had hastily copied years ago: Drain the cottage cheese in cheese cloth. Dry it out. Mix it with ricotta and feta cheese, but make sure that your *phyllo* dough stays moist. *Phyllo* dough, that fine, translucent substance that melts in your mouth when baked. The recipe continued: Crumble more feta. Mix with bread crumbs. Play around with the texture and the taste. No one had recorded the exact measurements for this recipe, assuming that the baker would understand the directions to do just that—play around with the texture and the taste. Beyond this recounting of the recipe which verbally had traveled from great-grandmother to grandmother to daughter to the next generation of granddaughters and great-granddaughters, young women—working side by side with the older women—had learned to bake these pies. As they baked and chatted and laughed, well before it became a fashionable concept, these women demonstrated the idea of mentoring.

Dampen the *phyllo* dough with a tea towel. I meticulously continued at my task. Layer and butter, butter and layer—the butter is your glue. As I continued, I thought of the generations upon generations of Macedonian, Greek, and Bulgarian women—Balkan sisters—preparing these pies.

Make sure that you skim the white substance from the butter; that's the salt. Don't forget the family secret: add a little bit of cornstarch and breadcrumbs to thicken the mixture.

As my fingers played with the dough, making layer upon layer of dough and cheese mixture, I was struck by the array of food items. On one side of the table, I could see a trio of Mediterranean-type food staples: feta cheese in brine, bitter black olives, and figs. They formed a dark background against the light brown, *pascha* bread with the dyed egg in the middle of the braided dough. *Pascha* meant pass-over, which symbolized the pass-over from death to life, from earth to heaven. Even though Passover was an Old Testament Jewish tradition, our family, comprised of Eastern Orthodox Christians, faithfully incorporated this *pascha* bread, which we called Easter bread, into our traditional Easter meal.

On the other side of the table sat a container of strawberries and pretzels waiting to be dipped in dark chocolate. Perched on the coffee table were beautifully decorated Easter baskets overflowing with chocolate candies, jelly beans, gum drops, decorated eggs, and a myriad of trinkets. Each basket would contain a little card or memento that reminded us of the reason for this celebration: "Christ is Risen! Truly, He is risen!" Generations of family members knew that response both in English and in the Slavic language: *Christos Vos Krese! Voistinu Vos Krese!*

I glanced around the room and chuckled as I noticed the ham, resplendent with pineapple rings and maraschino cherries, propped next to a casserole dish with rice pilaf. Who could possibly enter this kitchen and surmise the ethnic background of the cook?

I continued working with the dough, but now I focused on the spinach mix. Saute the leeks and spinach in olive oil and then mix it with the feta cheese. Make little spinach pies with the *phyllo* dough.

My cooking plans raced in my mind. When I was done preparing the spinach and cheese pies, I marinated the beef and pork. The only traditional meat dish missing was lamb; my mother always made the barbecued lamb, purchasing the meat fresh from a local ethnic butcher.

Mounds of strawberries for strawberry short-cake, apple pie with vanilla ice cream, and chocolate cupcakes with white icing would complete the meal. The kids loved chocolate cupcakes with white icing.

My Easter meal, so diverse, symbolized the blending of the all-American girl with deep-running ethnic roots and family traditions birthed in a remote, Macedonian village. Above the food and Easter baskets hung the most obvious reminder of that heritage: an elaborately handcrafted, belly-backed mandolin adorned with an inlaid mother-of-pearl butterfly in the center. This mandolin, over a hundred years old, arrived from Europe on the shoulders of my grandfather, Dimko Moisoff.

Like a camera, my eyes scanned the room taking a mental photo of each item, these special tokens of our Easter celebration which represented both Old and New World traditions. And I fondly thought of my relatives, especially Annastasia, my grandmother.

Chapter 1...
Escaping the Killing Fields

Mladi Kapetane   (My young captain)
Ot kude ide te vi?   (Where are you going?)
Ja idem za Balkana (I'm going to the Balkans)
Is borbi kurvavi.   (Where there is bloodshed.)

On a breezy April morning in 1895, the Stojanoff family celebrated. Mama Stojanoff had just given birth to twins: Elija and Annastasia. Papa Stojanoff, an impoverished priest in the local Macedonian Orthodox Church, had hurried home to witness this miracle of life. The labor and birth of the twins had been difficult, yet Antina, the midwife in this Macedonian village, had once again demonstrated her skill. Antina had proudly been there for many births in the Stojanoff family. As she lovingly washed the tiny babies, eight-year old Pero patiently waited for his introduction to his two new siblings. Antina gently placed Baby Annastasia in her mother's arms, and Baby Elija in the proud arms of his brother. Pero took one look at these two precious bundles, his brother and sister, and vowed that he would protect these two babies forever.

Joyous moments like these were few. In 1895, Bitola, Macedonia, was a European province of the Ottoman Empire, and most of the villagers had heard the horrific reports: By order of the sultan, Turkish Moslems were committing atrocities on Macedonian Christians.

"The time for an independent Macedonian state is now!" the men of the village clamored. "Restore Macedonia to her days of glory!" Macedonia the proud, ancient civilization that had birthed Philip and his son Alexander the Great, wallowed in oppression. The newspaper headlines caused terror, "Macedonian brothers are murdered on the roads and our Macedonian sisters are disgraced by the bloody Turk!"

As Macedonia cried out to her Balkan brothers for help, she found herself in the middle of their political desires. Bulgaria, Serbia, and Greece argued for acquisition of this territory landlocked geographically with Serbia to the north, Greece to the south, and Bulgaria and Albania to the east and west, respectively. These Balkan neighbors swore to help Macedonia, our "Brother Christians," against the oppressive Turks. Bone-chilling narratives surfaced of Macedonian Christians being forced to convert to Islam or face torture and ultimately death.

Macedonia's cries went unanswered as her Balkan brothers secretly met to attain their real goal: the partition of Macedonia.

Papa and Mama Stojanoff feared for the future

of their children, especially their sons. Their time for worrying about their children was short-lived. In 1896, as the Greco-Turkish War raged, Macedonia became the stomping grounds for skirmishes and Mama and Papa Stojanoff were tragically killed by Turkish soldiers. Genocide had found another home in this world.

It happened on a peaceful, Sunday morning following the church service. The Macedonian Orthodox Church in Bitola, Macedonia, where Papa Stojanoff served as a priest, was only a short distance from their modest home. With children in tow, Mama and Papa Stojanoff walked home, enjoying the warm sun and the quiet time together. From a distance Mama Stojanoff noticed what appeared to be a cloud of dust.

"Look over there," she pointed to her husband. "What is that in the distance, that cloud of dust? There's no wind to stir up the dirt. What can it be?" Papa Stojanoff squinted his eyes for a better look. "I don't know—wait a minute—it seems to be moving closer," he said.

Curiosity turned to horror when the couple realized that the cloud of dust was made by the hooves of rapidly approaching horses. Mounted firmly on the backs of these horses were turban-clad Turkish soldiers, menacingly waving silver objects in their hands.

"Pero! Take the twins and run! Run, Son, as fast as you can—run to the fields! Hurry! Hurry!" Mama Stojanoff screamed hysterically to her eldest son.

The twins, a little over a year old, started to cry

and frantically reached for their mother, but Pero, seeing the look in his mother's eyes, the look of a cornered animal, grabbed the twins, one in each arm, and ran with all his might. He glanced back just in time to witness the brutal murder of his parents by this marauding party of Turks.

Brandishing a scimitar (a curved sword used by Arabs and Turks) and bent on a mission for what the Turkish sultan had justified as a holy war, a Turkish soldier on horseback swooped down on the couple, and with one swift slice of that hideous weapon, the soldier beheaded Papa Stojanoff. As Pero looked on in horror, he witnessed the murderer proudly collecting his war trophy—the head of Papa Stojanoff, which he carelessly tossed into a basket. Hidden in the distance, the children had escaped death, but they could not escape the sounds of their mother screaming as she, too, was murdered. Had the circumstances been different, Pero would have hurried back to gather the desecrated bodies of his parents, granting them an Orthodox burial service with full honor and solemnity. But he couldn't think of that now; he could only think of survival for him and for his brother and sister.

By some great miracle, the lives of the three children had been spared. Pero knew that he had to keep his vow to protect his siblings. Soliciting the help of other villagers, Pero painstakingly made his way to the home of his maternal grandmother. There the three children attempted to live in peace in this land scarred by fighting.

The twins began attending one of the Macedonian

grammar schools in Bitola. There were several grammar schools in the village representing the various ethnic groups: Turkish, Greek, Serbian, and Bulgarian. In each school, the teachers told their students, all Macedonians, that they were not Macedonians. The Turkish grammar school teachers told the Macedonian children that they were Turkish; the Greek grammar school teachers told the Macedonian children that they were Greek. The Serbian and Bulgarian schools did likewise. For the most part, the twins received most of their education, which was minimal, in the Serbian-Macedonian schools. Politically, it was a difficult place to live. In 1906, the children's grandmother died. Annastasia and Elija, now almost eleven, were placed in an orphanage. Nuns of the Eastern Orthodox faith cared for all of the children in the orphanage. As Macedonia increasingly became a battlefield in the volatile political situation of the Balkans, more and more children were orphaned and the over-worked nuns had little time to maintain sanitary conditions, let alone provide the children with love and compassion.

Between 1898 and 1903, more than four hundred confrontations occurred between the Macedonians and the Turks. By 1911, the political situation, always volatile, exploded. More than 200 villages with 17,000 homesteads were completely destroyed. Genocide continued. The cry went up, "Macedonia for the Macedonians!" The stage was set for the Balkan Wars, two short wars fought for the possession of the territories of the Ottoman empire, including Macedonia. On October 18, 1912, the Anti-Ottoman League was formed, and Bulgaria,

Greece, and Serbia declared war on the Ottoman Empire. Once more, propaganda perpetrated the idea that the Balkan countries would help to release Macedonia from her bondage of slavery under the Turks, but freeing Macedonia was not their aim. Bulgaria and Serbia had already met secretly to make plans for the partition of Macedonia: Serbia would keep Skopje, the Macedonian capital, and Bulgaria would keep the areas of Thessaloniki, Bitola, and Veles. This powder keg in the Balkans escalated when Serbia and Greece, joined by Romania, signed a secret treaty for action against Bulgaria.

Austria-Hungary sided with the Bulgarians, and Russia, always the protector of her Macedonian and Serbian Orthodox brothers, tried to peacefully resolve the conflict, but failed. An article written by Dimitar Chupovski appeared in a St. Petersburg newspaper:

"Despite vigorous opposition by the Macedonians themselves, the partition of Macedonia will undoubtedly lead to internecine blood shedding among the allies."

On a sad, personal front, both of Annastasia's brothers disappeared, never to be seen or heard of again. Annastasia, now truly alone in the world, speculated that the young men, like so many others, had either been impressed into the army, or killed by the Turks, Greeks, Bulgarians, or Serbs. The nationalities of their murderers made no difference to her now. Unlike many of her countrymen, she felt no animosity to any particular ethnic group, somehow in her mind separating the vileness of the group from what she hoped was the goodness in the individual. Besides, this bleak life of war and death in Macedonia, now a routine, was all that she had ever known. She joined the multitude of weeping Macedonian women now widows, orphans, and childless mothers. Then as Providence would have it, a new love entered her life. She, so alone, embraced this new love in the form of an amiable musician from the village of Prilep, Macedonia. His name was Dimko Moisoff. A mutual friend had introduced Annastasia to this musician who made her laugh, something that she had not done in years. He would travel from his village in Prilep, Macedonia, to her city of Bitola to play his beloved mandolin with his orchestra. The orchestra, with its Macedonian-Greek sound, entertained the villagers with favorite folk songs and vibrantly-paced rhythms for dancing. For a brief evening, the Macedonian villagers forgot their woes, forgot that they were an oppressed people, and reveled in the intoxicating sounds of this orchestra comprised of a mandolin, accordion, guitar, clarinet, drums, and a flute-like instrument called a *frula*. She was almost eighteen; he twenty- six. There was an initial attraction, that first spark that draws two people together. But it was more than that. It was a mutual need and a mutual desire to somehow carve out a better life than the one handed to them. As the 1912 Balkan Wars raged, Annastasia Stojanoff of Bitola, Macedonia, and Dimko Moisoff of Prilep, Macedonia, were married in the local Macedonian Eastern Orthodox Christian church by Father Vladimir.

As newlyweds, they found themselves in the middle of the Balkan War crisis. One thing was certain: Dimko would have to join the army and fight and he, a carefree musician, did not want to fight; in fact, he wanted no part of that explosive corner of the world called the Balkans. Having few political sentiments, he saw the constant power struggles and the fighting as a waste of time and more tragically, a waste of lives. He hated war, so the decision was made. He would sail to America by himself to find a job and prepare the way for a new life for them. Having no family left in Macedonia, Annastasia would not be missed. Dimko had siblings, a brother and a sister who could follow later if they wished, but the situation in the Balkans called for immediate, drastic measures. A change had to be made if they were ever to be freed of the constant brutality of war. Annastasia was his life now, and he had to do whatever he could to protect their life together. He knew a few Macedonians from his village of Prilep who had settled in a tiny, Ohio community where the steel mills flourished. He knew nothing about the steel mills, only that they offered a means for an escape and a hope for a better life. In a year or two, he would send for his *zena* (wife). Before the coalition forces who occupied Macedonia forced the Ottoman Empire to seek an armistice on December 4, 1912, Dimko was on his way to America.

Chapter 2...Surviving a Boat Ride

Tamo daleko, daleko kraj moja   (Far away is my
    country)
Tamo je srce moje,   (Far away is my heart,)
Tamo je ljubav moja   (Far away is my love.)

After two long years away from her groom, the time for Annastasia's departure to America arrived. Though born and bred in a land-locked country, she approached the ship, docked in a Turkish port, with confidence. After losing both of her parents, her brothers, and spending years in an orphanage, how difficult could a boat ride across only *one* ocean be? Besides, her handsome husband would be waiting for her in America on the dock. Her Dimko with the wavy, black hair. Just the thought of him put a smile on her face, as she remembered putting her fingers through his abundant supply of hair; after all, they were newlyweds even if they had been separated for nearly two years. After working for a few months in the Detroit,

Michigan area, Dimko had finally reached his destination, the little steel mill town of Campbell, Ohio.

As she boarded the ship, her confidence waned. Never had she seen so many people! Even though she had lived in a city, Bitola, and not a dusty village, she was taken aback by the mass humanity entering the portal of the ship, only to be herded into the section labeled steerage. Fare for first or second class accommodations would be out of her reach. Somehow Dimko neglected to tell her this significant detail before he had embarked on his journey across the Atlantic. He had painted quite a different picture to her when he, always the optimist, had written:

"The ocean it *bee-a-u-tee-ful*, just like Lake Ohrid in Macedonia. You gonna see. *To bija dobro*—it be good." If the ocean was serene and beautiful, she didn't notice. She was too busy stepping out of the way of the rats that seemed to be everywhere. Sounds of individuals retching from the pitching of the ship, as well as the moaning of cholera-sufferers would cause her to cover her ears and sing one of her favorite Macedonian tunes, *Mladi Kapetane* (Young Captain), to stifle the pitiful sounds of suffering humanity. How ironic that her favorite song lamented the saga of a young sea captain who went to fight in the Balkan Wars. She made a vow to stay healthy and strong, no matter what. Nothing would prevent her from entering that land of opportunity, nothing would prevent her from seeing her beloved Dimko, now settled close to two years in the new country.

Numerous trips to the primitive toilets and washrooms were agonizing. Cold saltwater was the only means for keeping a minimal standard of cleanliness. The voyage was so horrific for her that she vowed never to travel by sea again. She had purchased a one way ticket to America. That was the final destination, nothing more; a landlubber she would remain for the rest of her life! She tried to recall the name of the *selo* or village where Dimko had settled. Then she chuckled.

"*Americanski* do not live in villages; they call the places *vhere* they live towns or cities," she giggled. "I *vill* have to remember to say city if I *vant* to sound like proper *Americanski* woman!"

Despite the substandard sanitary conditions on the ship, Annastasia willed herself to move about the ship. She started to meet and converse with many people. Slavic people of every clan, tribe and village imaginable seemed to be compressed into steerage. Like a motley colored tapestry, their attire boldly proclaimed their ethnic heritage: There were gypsies from Kossovo with bangles on their arms and ankles to match the gold in their front teeth; Serbians wearing baggy trousers, tri-colored cummerbunds, and pointed leather shoes called *opanke*, and the Croatian women, wearing muslin skirts delicately embroidered with red and white flowers, seemed to be flying through the air in a circle dance, called the *kolo*.

In an unusual display of solidarity, Macedonians joined with Greeks in a captivating folk dance played on a *koza,* a bagpipe made from goat's skin. Pressed in on all sides, the ocean companions were mesmerized by the leaps and twirls of the hanky-wielding lead male dancer as he shouted, *"Opa!"* In the midst of the most wretched sanitary conditions and rampant sickness, these feisty immigrants found moments of reprieve and pure joy in their music and their dancing.

While fascinated by this conglomeration of Balkan people, Annastasia did not limit her association to just her own kind; she became acquainted with a few Poles, Romanians, Italians, and Hungarians, and with a natural born talent for languages, she was able to converse with them. Thousands of miles from the American shore, she would experience firsthand the initial stirring of that great melting pot of people that would become Americans. Whether America wanted them or not, they were on their way!

Finally, she discovered and befriended a fellow Macedonian woman, Elena Spirkoff. Instead of focusing on the unsightly scenes on the ship, the two young women with a common language and similar background, pursued a more entertaining subject matter: talking about their lovers and husbands. From that moment on, until the boat docked, Annastasia bragged about her beloved Dimko.

"Chekaj! Vait till you see him—dark, tall, curly hair. *Ve* used to go for picnic in park, and I *vood* sit on blanket, and Oh, *boze moj* (my goodness!) how I *luf* to put my fingers through his hair," she giggled. "His name is Dimko," she proudly informed her fellow seafaring passenger. "He *vait* for me on the dock. He left Old Country two years ago to get job in America, *da* (yes), so he could send for me, his *zena* (wife). He's a musician, you know? *Da!* He

makes *bee-a-u-tee-ful* music with his mandolin, and oh, he can sing, he can dance—but his hair—I love his hair."

In conversation for much of the journey, the time passed quickly and the two young women found themselves entering New York Harbor with the indomitable Lady Liberty magnificently holding her torch to welcome them. Elena excitedly pointed to this striking American monument. Annastasia should have been impressed, and had she paused a moment, she might have even reflected on the symbolism of this famous landmark—*Liberty Enlightening the World*. But she was too immersed in her thoughts of seeing her beloved Dimko, and the opportunity to show him off to her seafaring friend delighted her.

About to embark on a new life in a great new country, Annastasia Stojanoff Moisoff tightly squinted her eyes to scan the dock, looking for her Dimko. When they last embraced almost two years ago, he was a handsome man with volumes of curly, dark hair. She was a trim woman, a size seven, with high cheekbones that accented her luminous, hazel brown eyes. This was the memory that each of them kept tucked away like a faded photograph. She carefully surveyed the dock looking for her man that fit this mental picture. He wasn't there, at least not the Dimko that she had remembered. Instead, there stood a balding, young man cautiously waving as he walked up the ramp of the boat. The two nervously made eye contact. As the truth of his identity dawned on her, she started exclaiming, "You're bald!" He, not missing a beat, shouted back, "You're fat-*Ti si debala!*" In the course of two years, she had grown from a size seven to a size fourteen! As her friend Elena waited to be introduced, an indignant Annastasia with her chin up walked a far distance from Dimko, pretending she didn't know him. In their wake stood a bemused Elena. Life in the New World had begun for them.

The year was 1914. Sadly Annastasia and Dimko, like so many others, would once again experience a war, not just any war, but a world war. This time, however, they would experience this war under the mighty protection of their new and powerful country, the United States of America. In spite of America's ever-growing involvement in this war, the couple had reason to rejoice: they had reached their destination and fulfilled their dream—a dream birthed in an old world. America was now their home.

When he left Macedonia, Dimko had little with him in terms of money. It's been said that most immigrants coming through Ellis Island carried at best, $20.00, a pittance that would later be cashed at the money exchange station on Ellis Island. Dimko's *denar* would be converted to one dollar bills in US currency. Dimko took special note of the face of President George Washington on the dollar bill, and he swallowed hard as he read the green lettering on the back of the bill, "IN GOD WE TRUST." This pittance, however, would pale against the real treasure that Dimko Moisoff had brought with him: his precious mandolin, inlaid with a large mother-of-pearl butterfly in the center and trimmed with rectangular pieces of mother-of-pearl that shined as they reflected the light. Not even protected by a case or covering, this belly-backed mandolin would survive years of musical use in the hands of several generations of Moisoff children. No matter what the circumstances, there would be music.

Dimko, after briefly working in the factories of Detroit, Michigan, permanently settled among a small pocket of Macedonian immigrants and other ethnic people in a little, but thriving, Ohio town geographically named East Youngstown—later renamed Campbell after Mr. James A. Campbell, president of the Youngstown Sheet and Tube Company. Meshed into that great melting pot of the world, the United States of America, these Macedonian immigrants became well acquainted with their multi-cultural neighbors, who similarly had disembarked on an American shore from such places as Italy, Romania, Greece, Poland, Yugoslavia, Czechoslovakia, and Hungary. The Youngstown Sheet & Tube Company was the draw, for here was opportunity in the thriving steel mills of America to make a go at the American dream. In the early 1900s, the plant advertised for willing workers, and Eastern European immigrants, African-Americans from the South, and Puerto Ricans readily responded. Youngstown, Ohio, was located 65 miles from Lake Erie and 35 miles from the Ohio River. Although situated a good distance from major waterways that made for easy transportation of steel, the discovery of deposits of black band iron ore and bituminous coal in 1845 made the area a prime location for the erection of nearly twenty-one blast furnaces that changed the once serene farming landscape into a major manufacturing works. To aid the industrial progress, the state of Ohio built the Pennsylvania-Ohio Canal system that connected all the major areas of the state. Between 1875-1920, the capacity of the blast furnaces was at 4,000,000 tons, thereby requiring hundreds of workers. European immigrants, desperate for work, found job security in the immense industrial world of the Youngstown Sheet and Tube Company. Dimko labored in one of the subsidiaries of this industrial giant, the Campbell Works. Named after company president James A. Campbell, the company boasted of a very productive coke plant and blast furnace. The work was hard, and when Dimko first caught sight of the blast furnace and its never ceasing heat, he swore that he had entered the portals of hell. But the work provided food on the table and a roof over their heads.

They purchased a company home with the backing of the all powerful steel company and Dimko, unable to afford an automobile, walked several miles to the mill every day, down the steep hill to the Campbell Works and back up to his home. Snuggled in this new life with a wife, a job, and a home, Annastasia and Dimko started their family. Their first baby, a son named Petar, did not survive and was buried in the small Orthodox cemetery in Campbell, Ohio. The close proximity of the cemetery to the grieving mother's home allowed for daily visits, which sadly seemed to extend the healing process of the suffering young mother. Since boys were so important to Macedonian-Greek families, this death was a terrible loss. But they were young, and the next four babies arrived at close intervals: Stella, Antina (called Annette), Eli, and Boris. After a brief and unexplained pause from childbirth, Annastasia, now approaching her late 30's, had two more babies: Ljubica *(lu bee sa)*, and eight years later, Wallace. A sister of Dimko, who had come to America a year after her brother and had settled in the Harrisburg, Pennsylvania area in an arranged Macedonian marriage, raised a family of ten children and christened her children with similar names that her brother and sister-in-law had chosen. The cousins would grow up knowing they had a counterpart and namesake living six hours away. Sadly, Dimko's sister, Spasia Moisova Angeloff, died at age thirty-four, stricken with pneumonia as she awaited the birth of her eleventh child. For the rest of his life, Dimko would unjustly blame his brother-in-law, Svetko Angeloff, for Spasia's death, convinced that her health had been undermined by giving birth to so many babies in such a short span of time, never connecting the fact that his own wife Annastasia, along with thousands of women of the 1920s, experienced the same lot in life.

Dimko labored in the hot, steel mill during the week, but on the weekends he played mandolin with a Slavic band (a conglomeration of Balkan people from Serbia, Croatia, Macedonia, and Bulgaria). The band's musical opportunities included picnics, church dances, and evenings at the cafes and taverns located near the steel mill. These taverns, overflowing with a myriad of ethnic people, provided a respite to the weary, overburdened steel mill worker in the Youngstown, Ohio area. Often serving as a gathering place, these immigrants who shared a similar cultural background could forget about their troubles, if only for a short while, and enjoy their ethnic songs and dances. The immigrants may have gladly turned their backs on their homeland in Europe, but their music was tucked away deep in their hearts and found fertile ground to grow in America. For Dimko, playing music was his first love, not merely a means to augment his meager income. In the community he was known for his talent, as well as his great sense of humor. An old, Balkan folk legend stated that the man from the circus and his monkey, often called the monkey grinder man, would not come to Prilep, Macedonia, for a few coins and laughs. The reason: the men from Prilep, or *Prilepcini,* were too funny themselves—funnier than any monkey! Even during serious times, he could find a way to bring humor into the situation.

In 1916, a major workers' strike occurred in the Campbell Works of the Youngstown Sheet and Tube. The men argued for a raise from their meager nineteen and a half cents an hour. When they were offered the paltry increase of twenty-two cents, 1,000 of the 7,500 workers rioted. Before the state militia arrived with 1,000 soldiers carrying machine guns, the mill laborers, minus any organized union, set fire to the mill. Dimko felt the need to show a solidarity with his co-workers, but he wouldn't participate in any destructive behavior. In fact, in the midst of the conflagration, he stumbled on a discarded gun which he brought home. As he entered the front door, he had a plan to turn this incident into a comical situation before his nervous wife. He marched into the room with his shoulders back, his chin up, and the gun hanging over one shoulder. Annastasia screamed with fear. Dimko boasted, "Look at me! Look at me! *Gledaj!* (Look!) I big *gazda* (boss)—everyone look at me and they *afrraid*. See." As he stated this, he kept marching back and forth across the room like a toy soldier. Annastasia grew suspicious.

"No, you no big person. You hate guns. *Vhat* you talk about?"He admitted the truth. He only picked up the gun because he thought that it would be one less dangerous weapon for the enraged mob to use. Even in that critical time, he managed to keep a sense of humor. Indeed, Dimko was a funny man and his children, all six of them, would inherit this legacy. But more importantly, he taught his children how to play the mandolin and sing the Slavic songs, although Stella, Boris (Bobby), and Ljubica (Libby) would be the children who took hold of that musical heritage as musicians, and Antina (Annette) as a folk dancer. Wallace, truly the most *Americanized* of the offspring, dabbled with the guitar. Each weekend, the Moisoff children would go to the local Macedonian dance, or *vecerinka,* to hear their father and his band play traditional songs and dances. In this tiny Ohio community, they had recreated the culture of the Old Country, minus the ethnic fighting.

Life was pleasant for many years, then 1929 hit

with the full impact of what the Depression did to large immigrant families. To survive, the older children needed to supplement the family's income. After working for a brief period as maids, the two eldest daughters, Stella and Annette, longed for a better life.

In a misguided attempt to help their daughter, as well as lessen the burden of so many mouths to feed in their household, the parents made secret plans for a marriage between Stella and a Macedonian man. What did it matter if their daughter and this boy barely knew each other, let alone love each other? This man was Macedonian and an Eastern Orthodox Christian, that in itself was a strong basis for a marriage, in their minds.

But these daughters, born and raised in America, understood what their parents with their Old World way of thinking did not: America was, indeed, the land of the free, and as young American women, these American daughters could choose to do what they wanted.

Stella, embittered by their actions, fled to nearby Akron, Ohio, located about fifty minutes from Campbell. Annette, after sowing a few wild oats, eventually followed her sister to Akron. There in that industrial community where the Goodyear Rubber and Tire Company was supreme, they eked out a living and a life of their own choosing.

The boys, Eli and Boris, were sent to the woods of Pennsylvania to work in Franklin Delano Roosevelt's Civilian Conservation Camps (CCC). Receiving a meager $1.00 a day, plus room and board and job training, this provision by President Roosevelt would forever endear him, as well as the Democratic Party, to these European immigrants who had received an opportunity to survive the Great Depression. Henceforth, they would be Democrats. It was for their posterity to think differently, politically speaking.

Ljubica (nicknamed Libby) and Wallace were very little at the time of this world crisis, and therefore, very unaware of the devastating financial tragedy that had overtaken the world. Ljubica, whose name means love, later recalled fond memories of making a Christmas tree out of old newspapers during those difficult times and having her older sisters, despite their personal problems, buy her little treats and pretty clothes. Libby would never forget the loving gestures shown to her by her sisters, often more loving and caring than the actions of her own parents. She idolized these two sisters, and developed a close, loving relationship with them that would last a lifetime.

Libby and Wallace, the precious babies in a large family full of love, were protected from the ugliness of the Depression. They were unaware of the lay-offs at the mill. Much too young to reason why so many men were home in the neighborhood, they simply enjoyed all the attention from family members and visitors. Besides, now their father had more free time to play his mandolin. The mandolin, his pride and joy, provided supplementary income during this financially devastating time. People always needed a place to release tension, and the local tavern hired him for a few bucks a night to play with his band. In this atmosphere of music and drink, the jobless steel mill workers could escape their problems for a brief time. Let the women worry and pray at home.

As the Depression raged, not only the Moisoff family, but hundreds of steel mill workers suffered financially. First of all, the once abundant supply of bituminous coal so desperately needed for the blast furnaces was almost depleted. To make matters worse, the Youngstown Sheet and Tube Company was in debt. The rated capacity of the steel mill had dropped to a low point of 13.4%. The company had close to $14,000.000 in cash and US securities, but debts and financial obligations were tremendous. Then in 1934, the Campbell Works installed a 79 inch continuous hot rolled strip and sheet mill. This was a saving feature for the mill. With the increase in automobile and steel manufacturing, the mill and its products were in demand. Productivity was once again on the rise. To solve the problem of diminishing resources, supplies were transported from the Great Lakes area via the railway system, which had now replaced the Pennsylvania-Ohio canal system. Ohio would become the second largest steel producing state in the nation. Campbell, along with many great American cities, had survived the Great Depression, and so had the Moisoff family. It was now time for laughter and music.

Chapter 3...
Painting a Family Portrait

There is a time for everything
and a season for every activity under heaven:
...a time to weep and a time to laugh.
Ecclesiastes

The Moisoff family was not unique in their struggle for economic survival during the Depression. Most Americans did everything and anything they could to survive those years, and consequently, panhandlers abounded. Many individuals had too much pride to resort to begging, so to raise the level of their panhandling, a token product was often offered: home made jam, cucumbers, tomatoes, even rags. One such entrepreneur approached Dimko on a sweltering, July afternoon. Dimko had been in the midst of a music practice with his orchestra when one of his children yelled, "*Tate, Hajde ide mo*—come quickly, someone is at the door." As he opened the door, he was greeted by a man, sweat beading on his brows, exhibiting several paintings of Jesus Christ. Tate quickly scanned the sequential array of paintings noticing *Jesus in the Manger, Jesus Destroying the Temple, Jesus in the Garden of Gethsemane*, and finally the *Crucifixion of Christ.*

The gentleman asked, "Sir, are you interested in buying one of my paintings? People tell me that I have quite a talent for painting the likeness of Jesus Christ, our Father."

Now Tate had this knack for answering a question with a witty life lesson. The man, out to make a buck, was about to receive his lesson.

"How much?" Tate inquired.

"I will sell you each painting for $3.00, that's a fair price for work of this quality. These are some of my best works of Jesus Christ, our Father," said the salesman. Tate quickly replied: "Only $3.00 for Jesus Christ, <u>our</u> Father? I tell you *vat*—I give you $15.00 for *vun* painting if you paint something else for me first." Now this response sent Mama Moisoff scampering to the door. She knew that Dimko would never pay $15 for a painting, even one of Christ. It wasn't that he was cheap, or even frugal. In fact, money meant very little to him. He would have generously and willingly given the man money. He just wanted him to be sincere, and for some reason, a man selling cheap portraits of what he called "Jesus Christ, our Father," just didn't seem sincere to Dimko.

"$15.00! Yes sir!" The salesman seemed to forget the heat as he ecstatically replied:

"Whatever you want me to paint, I'll paint. Just tell me!"

"Tate smugly responded, "I *vant* you to do painting of my father."

"Oh, that won't be difficult. Please take me to your father, Sir," the salesman could barely control his eagerness with the prospect of making a buck so close to consummation. Tate paused a second, played with his pipe and casually said, "*Vell*, he still be in Europe."

The salesman faltered for a second and then questioned, "Well, will he arrive in America say in the next few weeks?" Tate quickly responded, "No! He never gonna come here."

"Hmmm. That poses a bit of a problem," the salesman calculated. "Let me think. OK! I've got it! Maybe you have a photograph of him, and I can do a good likeness using that photograph?"

"No have photograph-no have *nut-ting*. You just paint my father."

"With all due respect, Sir, if your father is not here, and you don't even have a photograph of your father, how do you expect me to paint his portrait? I've never even met or laid eyes on your father," the perplexed salesman answered.

The reply came quickly, "*Vell*, you good painter, no? You never saw <u>our father </u>Jesus Christ and you paint him? So, you never see my father, you still can paint him, no?" The salesman gathered his portraits and with shoulders sagging, quietly walked away. Perhaps, in the beginning, a simple, "No, sir, we don't want any panhandlers or solicitors around here" would have sufficed, but Tate Moisoff always had a way of dramatizing the absurd, and in doing so, made life a little more vivid and meaningful for those around him.

Tate held strongly to the plain and simple truth that people shouldn't swindle each other. He had learned this lesson the hard way in the Old Country.

As a young boy, he and his buddy Tomo had devised a plan to steal eggs from a local farmer's chicken coop. The plan was that Dimko would go into the hen house and sneak his hands inside the coop and steal the eggs. Unaware that the farmer was watching his actions, Dimko stuck his hand into the coop. To his astonishment and pain, he was greeted with a whack from the farmer with a two by four. With hands stinging, he returned to his friend.

"Did you get yours?" the expectant Tomo asked.

"*Da*! Yes! Now go and get yours!" Dimko cunningly replied. Poor Tomo received the same treatment from the farmer without any warning from his friend Dimko. Life lesson: only take what is yours, and no more!

Chapter 4...Ordering Donuts

Memories are sweet.

The family gathered around the dinner table drinking coffee, the thick Turkish coffee served in gold and white demitasse with delicate, matching saucers. The Turkish coffee was strong and bitter, much stronger than a dark cup of Espresso. Strewn about the table were small plates of fresh green grapes, black olives, chunks of feta cheese, and thick slices of homemade bread that neutralized the strong taste of the feta. Mama decided that she needed to order some more groceries. She called the local grocers Caldrone's and Cioffi's to place an order, a common practice in those days. Now Mama Moisoff had a gift and a natural talent for learning languages. By mere association and conversation with her many ethnic neighbors, she could master their language. This woman of minimal education learned to speak Italian from her friend Mrs. Balasone, Greek from her association with Mrs. Pappas, Romanian from conversations with Mrs.Floko; in fact, Mama spoke seven languages quite fluently. English was not one of them. The complexity of the English syntax baffled her. Besides that, she often changed the context of a word. For some reason, she got it into her head that the word *okay* could be synonymously used for the word *donut*. As she placed her food order with the Italian grocer Mr. Cioffi, an accommodating man, the conversation sounded something like this:

"Hello. Caldrone's and Cioffi's Grocery Store, Mr. Cioffi speaking."

Mama: "Hello Mr. Caldrone's and Mr. Cioffi's Grocery Store—Mr. Cioffi, is *dat* you? *Dis* is me."

Mr. Cioffi, identifying Mama Moisoff's trademark accent, cheerfully responded, "Oh,

Good morning, Mrs. Moisoff. How may I help you?"

"Let me see, now. I *vant vun* loaf of bread, *donut*? I *vant* two dozen eggs—no, *vait* a minute—make that three dozen, *donut?* Then I *vant vun* head of cabbage*, donut?* A quart of milk, *donut*? You hear *vat* I say now, Mr. Cioffi? *Donut*? Oh, some cheese—I guess I *vant* provolone, if you please, *donut*! Thank you, very much, *donut*."

Mr. Cioffi: "Fine, Mrs. Moisoff, will there be anything else?"

Mama: *"Vell, da,* yes,—since you nice man and you *aska* me—maybe some bananas, yes, *da ,I vant* some of *dat*, too, *donut*? Goodbye."

As the family sat around the table, the delivery man from the customer-pleasing Caldrone's and Cioffi's grocery store arrived with the requested groceries, including dozens of donuts!

"*Vat* is *dis*?" a befuddled Mama inquired. "I don't *vant* these donuts! *Vat is* matter *vith* that man? I gonna call him back, *donut!* The family had a great laugh as they gathered around the dinner table with donuts aplenty!

The dinner table, large and brown with a Formica top etched with yellow daisies, was a place of much family interaction, both good and bad. While Mama was sweet, albeit prone to dramatics, Tate was fun-loving, but with a short temper. When people, in stereotypical fashion, label someone as having a fiery, Mediterranean temper, Tate certainly fit the description. Yet, never wanting to show physical abuse of any type, he found alternative releases for his anger. This time it was the white lace tablecloth.

He and Mama had a spat. Nothing serious, but he was mad. After releasing a barrage of Macedonian expletives, he glared around the room, resting his eyes on the first inanimate object that he could find: the white, lace tablecloth that covered the brown, dining room table. With great flair, he impulsively grabbed the tablecloth laden with dishes, food, and silverware and pulled the whole thing off, causing all the kitchen paraphernalia to scatter everywhere! Libby, entering the kitchen at that moment, saw her brothers running out, their salvaged food items in hand. Glancing quickly she noticed Mama's lace tablecloth on the floor amidst broken pieces of dishes. In confusion she asked, "What's going on here?" Her brother Bobby without missing a beat smugly replied, "Your father is trying to be a magician!"

No one said a word. Mama cleaned up the room with Libby and Wallace. Tate cooled down, and life went on as usual.

Chapter 5...
Speaking the Language

How did you came?
Did you drove?

Mama Moisoff was a very amiable and generous woman. Even though she was poor herself, she always thought that there were others less fortunate than she. Often she would traipse through the neighborhood offering the "less fortunates" baskets overflowing with fruit, vegetables, feta cheese, mouth watering Macedonian pastries, favorite Macedonian and Mid-Eastern dishes such as tocini pepriki (hot peppers and nuts), and a Mid-Eastern dish of cucumbers, walnuts, and buttermilk called taritura. When friends or relatives visited the Moisoff household, they never left empty-handed. Neatly wrapped packages of meat, vegetables, pastries, fruit, and candy, fondly called care packages, were lovingly shoved into their hands as they

walked out the door, a tradition that Mama successfully passed on to her daughters and granddaughters.

Because of her generosity and friendliness and
the vivaciousness of the Moisoff family, the house
was always full of guests. The household seemed to
vibrate with her gregarious laughter. Mama's typical
and friendly greeting to visitors as they entered her
modest home was, **"How did you came, did you
drrove?"**(drove pronounced as *drof,* rolling the r).
She never could get the syntax quite right, and no one
ever bothered to correct her. With her high cheekbones and sweet smile, she had a way of speaking
and asking questions that never offended anyone.

A male friend of the family, who had a problem
with perspiration odor, once visited the Moisoff
home coming directly from the steel mill. Mama
Moisoff naively questioned him:

"Hmm," she sniffed, "You smell *tirred. Vere* you
rrunning?"

The next time that the young man visited the
Moisoff home, he cleaned up first.

"See Mrs. Moisoff, I took your advice," he said.
"I'm all clean and fresh now." She sweetly replied,
"I *no vember* telling you *dat*." (instead of I don't
remember.) In any case, the visitor was totally smitten with her sweetness and her quaint, if inaccurate,
expression.

To make matters more comical, Mama seemed
to associate herself with friends who had the same
language difficulties as she.

Once she and a Croatian friend made a trip to the
insurance office where Mama's friend made a

payment. In typical business fashion the man concluded the conversation with, "Goodbye and thank you."

"You're *walkin*," replied Mama's friend (instead of you're welcome).

"No, Ma'am. I'm not walking. I have a car parked just around the corner," said the insurance man.

"Oh, that be nice that you have car. Goodbye, thank you and you *walkin*." Mama's friend innocently responded.

"No, Ma'am. I am not *walking,* I will be driving my car," the man answered, this time a bit more emphatically.

"*Allrright* already. *Dobro* (Good) for you. *Drof* your car if you *vant*," interjected an impatient Mama. "We be going now."

The man made one last gallant effort at pleasantries, "It's been wonderful doing business with you ladies. Thank you."

Mama's friend sweetly responded, "You're *walkin*." Abbot and Castello and their "Who's on first" routine never sounded as confusing!

On November 26, 1941, at age 47, Mama finally received her Certificate of Naturalization, thus attaining American citizenship. This achievement, occurring seventeen years after her husband had received his naturalization papers, came with much effort and difficulty. She proudly displayed her certificate saying, "G*ledaj* (look), you see right here," pointing to the signature on the certificate. "The Deputy Clerk of Mahoning County of the Common Pleas Court signed this paper. He very important man and now I citizen of United States of America. *Gledaj-* you see the seal? It's raised, that be *verry* special."

Perhaps to show off just how much of an American she was, she offered to tutor one of her Slovak friends, Mrs.Barliak, who similarly was struggling with passing the test for this coveted certificate of naturalization.

After diligently working for many weeks with Mrs. Barliak, who had much difficulty understanding the language, let alone comprehending the significant historical developments of the United States, Mama took her nervous Slovak friend by the hand and proudly presented her to the Deputy Clerk, the designated proctor at the Naturalization Office in Youngstown, Ohio.

The coveted prize, American citizenship, dangled precariously before the struggling Mrs. Barliak, who try though she might, could not remember the items that they had painstakingly studied over the past several weeks. Question after question she labored, getting one answer correct, missing the next one. The Deputy Clerk kindly, but firmly said to Mrs. Barliak, "Ma'am, if you miss one more question, I will, unfortunately, have to fail you on this test for your American citizenship, for obviously, you do not know enough about this country. So now I will ask you one last question, "Who sewed the first American flag?"

By this time, Mrs. Barliak's composure was gone. With great flare, she looked the deputy in the eye and shouted, "*Kittsy vraus!*"

"What did you say? Please repeat that, Ma'am. Kittsy-Betsy? Vraus-Ross?" questioned the Deputy Clerk hearing something remotely close to the correct answer and truly wanting this woman to succeed.

Once again, this time with great disdain, Mrs. Barliak shouted, "*Kittsy Vraus!*"

"Yes! Yes! Betsy Ross! That is correct Ma'am!" he exclaimed. "You passed!" *Kittsy vraus* was interpreted as Betsy Ross. What that unsuspecting deputy did not comprehend was that he had just been emphatically told to "Go to the devil!" in Mrs. Barliak's native language. Mama and Mrs. Barliak demurely left the courtroom, precious Certificate of Naturalization in hand, and once out of earshot of the official, snickered all the way home, "*Kittsy vraus*...Betsy Ross!"

Chapter 6...
Jumping in Corn Fields

Trust in the Lord, with all your heart,
And lean not on your own understanding.
In all thy ways acknowledge Him,
And He will direct your paths. (Proverbs 3: 5,6)
King James Version.

Having raised four older children, Mama and Papa at this stage of their lives should have settled into a quiet, peaceful routine, but all that changed with the births of their last two children, Vasso (Wallace) and Ljubica (Libby—sometimes called Ljuba). Born seven years apart to Mama and Tate, who by this time were in their late thirties and mid-forties respectively, this devilish duo ruled the nest! Perhaps the aging parents thought that this behavior represented the new philosophy of American thinking, or perhaps they were just completely tired out. Whatever the reason for the releasing of the parental reigns, Libby and Wallace, incredibly spoiled by their aging parents, used every means possible to manipulate their parents into getting what they wanted. Old World thinking and discipline were gone. Libby, the elder of the two and definitely the ring leader, always threatened to jump out of the second story bedroom window if she didn't get her way. Using this trump card, Libby totally manipulated her gentle mother into giving her everything that she wanted. In complete exasperation, Mama Moisoff visited the local public school guidance counselor to see if he could give any advice as to what she should do with her Ljuba, whose name meant love in the Slavic language. This whirling dervish of a little girl exemplified anything but love.

Mama Moisoff, by this time carrying a good deal of extra weight, waddled into the office of the guidance counselor at the local public school and pleadingly said, "Mr. Pacella, I don't know *vat* to do *vith* my Ljuba. *Lele, Boze* (Oh, lord). If I tell her not to do something—she says she gonna do it anyway, and if I try to stop her, she tells me that she *vill* jump out of the *vindow* upstairs and you know Mr. Pacella, that *vindow* is two, how do you say, two *stores* up!"

The highly educated public school counselor emphatically stated, "Mrs. Moisoff, you must use psychology on your daughter."

Mama Moisoff inquired, "*Vat's* this, *si-kol-gy? Ne rasumi?* I don't understand."

Mr. Pacella: "Psychology. Well, it means, more or less...well, for example, it means..." stammering as he looked at Mrs. Moisoff's confused face, "You see, your daughter Libby really doesn't mean to carry out what she says."

"She don't?" asked Mama Moisoff.

"No, Ma'am. She's merely bluffing. So, if she tells you she is going to jump, you use psychol—well..er... you just call her bluff. Do you understand bluff?"

"Bluff? Like a cliff? She gonna jump off cliff?" Mama responded with incredulity.

"No, Mrs. Moisoff, a bluff is...well. OK. Let's see. The next time your Libby says that she is going to jump, you tell her to go ahead and jump. I guarantee that she will not do it."

"You *vant* me to tell her to jump? I don't know, Mr. Pacella. You smart man, but I don't know."

"Trust me, Mrs. Moisoff. I work with all types of difficult children. It's my job to know how to deal with these children. Your little Libby is no exception."

With great new confidence in her parenting skills, Mama walked out of the Penhale Avenue Elementary School office eager to test this new thing called *psychology* on her Ljuba. Her opportunity came quickly. It was dinner time, and Libby was upstairs completely involved in playing with her toys. Mama called, "Ljuba, it's time to eat. Come downstairs."

Libby whined, "No, I wanna play. I'm not coming downstairs." Mama immediately responded with firmness, "That's enough. *Dosta*. You stop playing right now and come downstairs to eat!" Libby, true to form, said, "If you don't let me keep playing, I'm gonna jump from the window!"

Mama confidently climbed the stairs, sauntered

to the window, and opening it widely said, "Go ahead, jump!" Once more, the impish Libby threatened, "I mean it. I'm gonna jump! You'll be sorry!" Mama, confidence somewhat dwindling, managed a final, "*Vell* then, go ahead—you jump! See if I care."

What followed were several minutes of absolute mayhem! Libby jumped from the window of a second story bedroom! She miraculously landed smack dab in the middle of the soft cornstalks growing in the neighbor's garden. Mr. Balasone's garden, full of ripened cabbages, squash, and a bountiful corn field, was the perfect spot for a safe landing. Mama started screaming "*O! Boze moj! O Boze moj!* (Oh, my God! Oh, my God!) and in her state of confusion, mistakenly called the Campbell Fire Department.

As sirens blared towards the Moisoff's home, neighbors by the dozens poured out of their homes. Libby, unscathed from her jump out of the second story window, walked out of the garden and back into the house. Mama Moisoff never took the advice of an American educator again!

~

Tate Moisoff, similarly, had his woes with the American educational system and more specifically, its language. Unlike the simplistic format of his native, Macedonian dialect, the English language for him consisted of too many inconsistencies. One of the culprits was the word *register*. Little Libby, who was bi-lingual, but leaned more proficiently towards her Macedonian language, had difficulty comprehending the definition of the word *register*. After repeatedly missing this word on a vocabulary test and refusing to pronounce this word in English, Libby was told to bring one of her parents to school. Since Mama absolutely refused to have anything more to do with the American school system after the second story window fiasco, Tate, grumbling all the way, visited the teacher. If the teacher thought that she was going to have an ally in Mr. Moisoff, she was greatly mistaken. Tate Moisoff did not go against one of his own in public. After explaining the situation to him, the teacher confidently waited for his chastisement of Libby. Instead, the teacher received a lesson in languages:

Tate: "*Vat* is this *vord-rregister?* Thickly rolling his r's he complained, "You *rregister* to vote. You put your money in a cash *rregister*. You *rregister* a thought in your head. You have a *rregister* on the wall, no? You know, *vere* the heat comes out?

"Indeed, Mr. Moisoff, but, uh, well, you see..." stammered the once confident teacher.

"No, I don't see! V*at* you talk about? Now *gif* me just *vun* meaning for that *vord rregister*, Tate emphatically requested.

"Well, Mr. Moisoff, there really isn't one definition, and I don't know what to say to you," was her reply.

"*Vell,* you *surrre* had lot to say before about *rregister,* and if you don't know *vat* to say now, *vat* you expect my little Ljuba to know, eh?" he sarcastically questioned.

The closest Macedonian word that he could find

to match register was *reshetketa*. Singularly purposed, the word meant "to release heat." It didn't grant you permission to vote for a political figure on election day since you were *registered*. It didn't open its drawer to receive money like a cash *register*. A thought, however profound, didn't *register* in your mind. Simply stated, a *register*—or what he called a *reshetketa*—released heat. Single purposed words, according to Tate, made sense out of life. They provided him with clear-cut directions and flowed placidly in his world of black and white, not gray.

Tate Moisoff, with little Libby in tow, left the school that day providing the befuddled teacher with something to ponder for her next teaching lesson on vocabulary words.

Nevertheless, even though Tate stood by his daughter and her problems at the *Americanski* school, he recognized that he and Mama needed some help in controlling their high energy, strong-willed daughter. While Mama tended to the baby, Libby continued to get herself into mischief. When the public school system didn't help, the frustrated parents pursued another source: the local Baptist Mission Center called Bethel House or House of Bread. Providing a safe place for the neighborhood children to go on Saturdays and after school, the little missionary, founded in 1919 by Rev. Robert Hughes of the Hazelton Baptist church, introduced the children to scouting, arts, crafts, and Bible stories. For some of the children, whose only religious instruction consisted of participating in a mass or liturgy spoken in various European tongues, these

Bible stories of David and Goliath and Abraham and of the miracles of Jesus, were brand new and the children were awe-struck by them. Additionally, instructors at the Bethel House were tremendous resources for teaching English to the children of immigrant parents. Records show that some 3,300 immigrants achieved American Naturalization and Citizenship through the aid of the Bethel House and its sister organization, the Neighborhood House. While Libby, born in America, didn't need to earn her citizenship, Mama and Tate felt that this place, while not necessarily the definitive answer, provided a respite from the consuming job of managing her. Staunch Eastern Orthodox people, at least in tradition, Mama and Tate recognized the need of a higher power and the Baptist Mission Center was providing a means to tap into that power.

"*Ako Bogda*, Lord willing," Mama Moisoff mumbled as she made the sign of the cross three times, packed a little sack lunch with green peppers, cheese, and freshly baked bread, and sent Libby to the Center accompanied by a throng of neighborhood friends. On cold days, Mama gave Libby two hot potatoes to put in each of her coat pockets, thus keeping her hands warm as she walked to Bethel House located just a few streets from her home. That little mission center would provide Libby with an anchor of strength that would equip her for the rest of her life. She didn't know then just how much strength she would need for the trials ahead. Even as she remained an Eastern Orthodox woman for most of her life, she would always remember one of the

Bible verses that she learned by memory at the Baptist Bethel House, "Trust in the Lord with all your heart, and lean not on your own understanding; in all thy ways acknowledge Him, and He will direct your paths" (Proverbs 3: 5, 6).

Chapter 7...
Surviving Infamous Days

My Country tis of Thee
Sweet land of liberty
Of thee I sing.
Henry Carey

December 7, 1941—Day of Infamy! Every household in America was glued to the radio as President Franklin Delano Roosevelt announced, "America was suddenly and deliberately attacked by naval and air forces of the Empire of Japan. We will gain the inevitable triumph, so help us God."

In the days that followed, Mama and Tate Moisoff wept as their beloved President declared war on Japan. It was the right course of action in their opinion; they never disputed his decision. Yet, for them, war and destruction evoked too many painful memories of Macedonia and the ongoing fights in the Balkans. Although Mama Moisoff never talked about the horrible massacre of her parents in Macedonia, she would often tell her children when they asked her why she came to America, *"Ve* tired of *var* (war). *Alvays* the *var. Ve vant* peace. *Ve* come to America. *Vat*'s so much to say about *dat*? *To bija dosta* (That's enough). They equated America with security, safety—peace. To challenge those staples that lay within America's mighty borders was unthinkable. But Japan had done the unthinkable! While Dimko had managed to evade serving in the military forces of Macedonia, he and Mama, now proud naturalized American citizens, watched as their grown sons and one daughter, Antina, joined the Armed Forces. As was often the case with immigrants, the Moisoffs were a patriotic family. Ironically, Mama Moisoff had obtained her Certificate of Naturalization only a few weeks before the tragedy at Pearl Harbor had occurred. Dimko had been a naturalized citizen for years. Calling America their home was to them a privilege and a blessing. Their grandchildren would later recall some of their earliest memories of "Baba and Dedo" Moisoff celebrating the Fourth of July with the American flag flying faithfully on the front porch. Of course, there was always a European flavor to the celebration. Tate would play his mandolin and there would be singing and folk dancing in the backyard. With great anticipation, everyone watched the lamb roasting on the spit in the backyard. Each family member, from the oldest to the youngest, would receive a plate with a large portion of the lamb, chunks of feta cheese, black olives, Slavic bread called *pogacha* which was broken off and not sliced, and a large handful of fresh, green onions. The dessert consisted of delicious Macedonian pastries, green grapes, and watermelon. The family's Fourth of July celebration may not have included hot dogs, corn on the cob, and apple pie—but it was a celebration of America, nevertheless.

Because of their love and appreciation of their new country, there was no question concerning duty or loyalty, or even grumbling for that matter, when a declaration of war by a beloved president had been issued. The older boys, Eli and Bobby, went off to war. Antina (Annette) made her family proud by being one of the first women in the area to become an officer in the WACS. She was stationed in England and experienced firsthand the fierce bombing of London by the German *Luftwaffe*. Years later at her death, it was Annette's request to be buried with full military honors and in military uniform. Stella the eldest daughter, so steeped in the Macedonian culture as a child, married Donald Drumm, a man as un-ethnic as apple pie. Still bitter from the attempt of her parents to marry her off, Stella separated herself as much as possible from the Macedonian people for several years. A healing process was necessary and her marriage to Donald Drumm, a wonderful man who would bless her with a tremendous life and a beautiful family, was just the balm that she so desperately needed.

Like any other American family with loved ones in the service at this time, the Moisoffs worried and prayed about their sons and daughter overseas. It was teenager Libby's job to write to her brothers and sister, and in doing so, kept her worried parents informed. Libby would later complain that she had written so many letters to her brothers and sister overseas, as well as other servicemen, that her hands and joints would cramp. She imaginatively proclaimed herself as the original inventor of the concept of "tennis elbow."

While Tate Moisoff worried silently, Mama was emotional. She always imagined the worst possible situation. Close to the worst happened. When the war began, son Eli served his military duty as a paratrooper. He joked with the family telling them that he didn't want to join the army because they walked too much and he had flat feet. Stationed in Belgium with the 101st Airborne Division, Eli was being transported by glider across an open area when the Germans fired on his unit. Hit in the right shoulder by the volley of machine guns, Eli was sent home to the States to a veteran's hospital in Virginia for treatment. The injury was so severe that he almost lost his right arm. After receiving a shot of penicillin every hour for four months and undergoing months of rehabilitation, Eli adequately recovered, although this injury would always plague him. But his parents, particularly his mother, had dismal hopes for his ability to lead a productive life after his injury. Believing that he would need help in making a living, Mama and Tate made plans for his future when he came home from the war.

Chapter 8...Buying a Store

Macedonian Nursery Rhyme

Kads Babo batice   (Here is Grandma)
Napre na Babo vretence! (Everything is driving her
*   crazy!)*
Isi kala police   (She calls the police)
Doslo kuce popopalo!   (The dog is driving her nuts!)
Doslo mace popopalo! (The cat comes in driving her
*   nuts!)*
Ke mi vickni Tate, Brate (So she calls her husband and
*   her brother)*
Svreech se vo Grcite!   (Hide behind the Greeks!)
Eto ide Trseteh!   (Here comes the Turks!)
Ke mi bara parite   (Go look for money.)
Pukni tenjereto   (She has beans cooking on the stove)
Istodi gravo!   (They boil over since they went looking
*   for money!)*
(tickle, tickle, tickle) ˙

The war ended, and the soldiers came home. Annette by this time was engaged to Walter

Cologie, a large, soft-spoken man of Polish ancestry, but very *Americanized* having grown up on an Ohio farm. The concept of being *Americanized* was a big one in the family with both negative and positive connotations. Positive in that the family was proud to be American. Negative in the connotation that *Americanized* to them suggested a lack of roots, traditions, and cultural heritage. *Americanized* people were often called "cake-eaters" in a derogatory way by some Slavic people. Cake-eaters suggested that those people, in situations of hospitality, offered only cake, never a full meal. With the Slavic person's love of great food and a great capacity for giving, this would be seen as a great shame according to Slavic tradition. No one ever left a Slavic home hungry, or without a package of goodies to share with his family at home. Both Walter and Donald were *Americanized*, perhaps even bordering on "cake-eater" status, but they were received and loved by the family, nevertheless, and in the years to come, became one with the Slavic culture, in the family's opinion.

Annette and her new husband Walter followed sister Stella and brother-in-law Donald and settled in the Akron, Ohio area, a few streets apart from each other. The brothers-in-law began life-long careers working for the Goodyear Tire and Blimp Company of Akron, Ohio. The smell of the factory and burning rubber became a familiar odor that permeated the air surrounding their homes. Once a visitor to Stella's home made a snide remark concerning the pungent odor coming from the rubber factory. Stella defensively retorted, "Don't knock it. That smell—it's our bread and butter. As long as you can smell rubber, then things are booming in this town. No smell, lookout Akron, Ohio!" It was a prophetic statement.

Boris "Bobby" Moisoff married, had a son, and settled in the Youngstown area, working and playing music on the side. He organized a three-man orchestra that produced a large sound consisting of a mandolin, guitar, and an upright bass. But Mama and Tate were concerned about Eli and his ability to recover from his war injuries. Wishing to provide a living for their son, they bought a little home on Devitt Avenue with a store front. The idea was that Eli could come home and make a living from this little store. The family would live in the rooms above the store. Eli thought differently.

Eli's recovery in the veteran's hospital in Virginia proved to be a blessing for him. There he met and fell in love with a true Southern belle, Louise, who worked as a bookkeeper at the veteran's hospital. Definitely *Americanized* and a cake-eater to be sure, so much so that she changed his name to Bill, pronouncing it in two syllables as *Be-eel*. Her thinking was that the name Eli was too ethnic sounding. Louise's family, the Beverly's, were one of the first families of Richmond, Virginia—a status that made them a world apart from their new Macedonian in-laws with their ethnic traditions and Old World way of thinking. For them, these Macedonian immigrants were too loud, too many, and definitely too foreign. Reciprocally, the Moisoff relatives had difficulty accepting Eli's wife at first. However, as a family they could never close their hearts, or not extend their open arms to others. Thus, in due time, they warmly received this daughter-in-law even though it meant having their son Eli, a.k.a. *Be eel*, move to the South, develop a deep Southern accent, and refer to the rest of the family as "Ya'll!"

Every summer, in later years, the family would make the trek to Richmond, Virginia, to visit Uncle Eli (Bill) and his family. His two daughters, Brenda and Beverly, would introduce their relatives to their Southern neighbors in this manner: "Hey ya'll, we want you to meet our cousins—they're Yankees." The Yankee cousins whose grandparents had arrived in this country close to a half century *after* the Civil War, always found these introductions amusing.

When Eli's daughters visited "up North" with their grandparents, Tate "Dedo" would proudly walk them through his backyard pointing to all the trees and telling the girls that he had brought these trees as seedlings from the Old Country. The story was highly improbable, but the girls were mesmerized by their grandfather's talent for weaving a tale. The girls loved to hear the stories from this beloved man typically dressed in a white T shirt, old pants, and an old hat that a train conductor might wear. But contrasting his unfashionable clothes, he looked quite the cosmopolite as he held, European style, a cigarette in a fancy, gold cigarette holder, and as he told his stories—sagas from the Old Country—he emphatically moved his hands. With his flair for music, drama, and humor, he could captivate an audience no matter how large or what their age.

Often, he would bounce his giggling grandchildren on his knee as he held them captive with the tale of *Kads Baba* (Here Grandma). In this Macedonian nursery tale, the narrator rhymes nonsensical Macedonian phrases about a grandmother going nuts in a comedic way over the cat and the dog. The nursery rhyme takes on a political overtone as it admonishes, "Hide behind the Greeks! The Turks are coming!" At the end of the rhyme the grandmother, who has gone to look for money, leaves her beans boiling over on the stove. When Dedo Moisoff got to the part about the beans boiling over, he would grab a grandchild or two and tickle them. After regaining their breath, the children, both the Southern cousins along with their Northern cousins would yell, "*Jos jedan, Dedo*! (Once more, Grandfather!) Once again, he would start, "*Kads Babo, batice*..." The children all adored their beloved *Dedo* (Grandfather) Moisoff.

~

Bill, Louise, and their family remained in Virginia where Bill began working for Louise's father who owned a trucking business. Mama and Tate Moisoff now owned a grocery store, or at least the makings of one. But they never operated it effectively as a store. They were poor businessmen, giving away more than they earned. Mama, Tate, Libby, and Wallace lived in the rooms above the store. These were the years that Libby and Wallace went absolutely wild. Unable to control these two when they were children, the aging parents certainly could not control this incorrigible duo as they entered their teenage years.

Wallace pretty much followed older sister Libby in her escapades. Both Libby and Wallace would have scars for the rest of their lives from battles the two of them had with razor blades! After one particularly injurious battle, Mama had to take the dueling pair to the emergency room to get stitches.

The emergency room doctor dressing the children's wounds questioned Mama: "Ma'am, what is going on here? How did the two of them get these cuts?"

Mama: "*Vell*, you know how kids are. They *vatch* in the movie picture how they have...how do you say...*sworrd* fight... you know. They take the razor blades and *vell*...they play!"

The doctor exclaimed, " Play? How do they play? Ma'am, I'm sorry, but this just isn't playing. This is very serious! They must stop! They're going to kill each other!"

Mama responded to this admonition as if this suggestion was a totally new idea to her: "Oh, my! Ljuba! Vasso! You stop at *vunce*! *Dosta*!"

In spite of the warnings from the emergency room doctor, the devilish duo would have many more harrowing escapades for a few more years.

~

When Libby got into trouble at school, which was often, she simply intercepted any notes and phone calls from the school, since her mother and father had difficulty with the English language. Close to her senior year, Libby was suspended from school. She had boldly engraved her name on a brand new sewing machine that had just been purchased for the home economics class. When the teacher, whose first name was Hildegarde confronted Libby with her evil deed, Libby, always sassy, replied, "Well, Hildegard, I just thought I'd make sure I knew which sewing machine was mine."

This was prompt and just cause for a three day suspension from high school. Libby had one of her girlfriends forge the signature on the note that had to go home. And she had her girlfriend's mother, another Macedonian immigrant who spoke absolutely no English, impersonate Mrs. Moisoff. Somehow the scheme worked without Mama and Tate ever finding out about the incident. However, Libby's heart was now removed from the school scene. Returning to school after the suspension, she made up her mind to finish school as quickly as possible, and being a bright girl, she rushed through her required courses and graduated a year ahead of her high school class.

In spite of the disciplinary mar on her record, she had offers for college because she was academically smart as well as athletic, but her father totally opposed any college opportunities. "*Vat* you need this college for?" he questioned. "You gonna get married—have babies—be a good *zena* (wife). That's *vat* girl must do. Don't talk no more of this college. I no hear *nut-ting* more of this." Mama

71

supported Tate in this thinking. Case closed.

Libby took a job in a local bakery and tried her hand at cake decorating for a while. But this job was not nearly challenging enough to quiet her adventurous spirit. She seemed bent on a path of destruction when something captured her heart that would change her life...MUSIC!

Chapter 9...Playing Tambura

Sviraj tamburasi! (Play tamburitzans!)

The Southern Slavic people have their own unique, musical instrumentation. It's called *tamburitzan* music. Not to be confused with a tambourine, *tamburitzan* instruments are part of a stringed orchestra. An individual instrument is called a *tambura,* and collectively, the instruments are called *tamburitzan* instruments, played by *tamburasi* (musicians). Each instrument has its own unique and lyrical name such as *prim or bisernica, brac, bugaria.* Consisting of several guitar-sounding instruments in the orchestra, it provides a delightful sound for singing and dancing. Libby in her early teens began playing these instruments.

It started with her observance of her father and his band practicing three times a week at their home. When the men would leave, Libby would pick up the mandolin and pluck out a few tunes. Her father never encouraged her in this endeavor since he

73

didn't think that girls should play music. When she tried to show off her musical talents to her mother, Mama Moisoff gruffly responded, "Better you try to sound like Shirley Temple. Now that's somebody!"

Nevertheless, she was undaunted in her musical yearnings. She found an old guitar at the city dump, patched it up, and experimented with some chords. Once her fingers touched the strings of a guitar, girl or not, she would not be silenced!

To kick off her musical career, she joined a country western band whose members included such names as Butterball, Ida Mae, and Scotty. For $10 each weekend, she belted out tunes and strummed chords on a guitar until her throat was hoarse, and her fingers ached with blisters from underdeveloped calluses. As the jobs continued, those necessary calluses formed, but unfortunately, her sweet-sounding, soprano voice experienced vocal damage due to a lack of proper vocal training and care. In smoky, noise-ridden music halls and taverns, the antiquated microphones inadequately amplified her voice. With each decade, her vocal range got deeper. By the end of her music, and later radio career, that once soprano voice would be a deep, resonating alto, almost bordering on bass-like qualities. The volume, however, never lessened.

Libby did more than sing and play an instrument. She was a natural born comedienne and had a stage presence with a knack for connecting with her audience. But in the late 1940s, in industrialized and predominantly ethnic Youngstown, Ohio, country western music was not that popular. The community definitely had a European flavor to it with Greeks, Italians, Serbians, Croatians, Macedonians, Russians, Romanians, Hungarians, Slovaks, Poles, Hispanic, Irish, Germans, and other ethnic groups living in this area. There was also a large African-American culture emerging in the area, essentially due to the steel industry and the opportunity to work; however, the two diverse cultures, European and African-American, existed separately, albeit peacefully.

A large population of Southern Slavs who thoroughly enjoy tamburitzan music exists in the United States. The music has international appeal. After dabbling with the country western experience, Libby returned to her ethnic roots and began playing tamburitzan music professionally. For this, she gave up her guitar and joined a group of friends and received musical instruction for the tambura. The teens, Chito, Dorothy, and Katherine— all Serbian, except for Libby, who was Macedonian, even though she attended the Serbian Orthodox Church, hopped on a bus from Campbell, Ohio, and traveled to Youngstown to take lessons from a prominent tamburitzan player in the Youngstown area named George Skrbina. The teens knew Mr. Skrbina and his son Rudy from the church. Musicians from the Serbian church would play music on Saturday nights, many times receiving ones, fives, tens, and twenty-dollar bills as tips.

These tips were not placed in their pockets, but were ripped and shoved onto the tuning pegs of the instruments, or moistened with saliva and plastered on the musicians' foreheads in a gesture of appreciation. Often on a Sunday morning, these dollar bills would surface, holes and all, in the Sunday morning offering plate during the Orthodox liturgy. Their talent was music, and they gave their firstfruits back to God.

Never inquiring which instrument of the tamburitzan orchestra the teens wished to play, Mr. Skrbina assigned instruments according to what he deemed created the best sound for an orchestra. Libby, with her guitar background, was great with rhythm and chords, so he gave her a *bugaria*, a guitar-like instrument that consisted of a D string, an A string, and two F sharp strings, tuned an octave apart. Along with the upright bass and the tamburitzan cello played with a pick, this instrument kept the orchestra rhythmically stable. It also gave Libby great leverage to move around and "work" the audience, and work them she did!

Libby was on her way to an illustrious music career that would span close to sixty years and provide her with many accolades, including a performance at the Inaugural Ball of President Jimmy Carter. But love and romance put a temporary pause on her orchestra days.

Chapter 10...
Finding and Losing Love

I'll see you in my dreams
I'll hold you in my dreams
Someone took you out of my arms
Still I feel the thrill of your charms
Lips that once were mine
Tender eyes that shine
They will light my way tonight
I'll see you in my dreams

Sung by Vaughn Monroe
Words and music Gus Kahn and Isham Jones

Libby, of all the Moisoff children, was and is the most colorful. Her persona was always bigger than life. Libby is my mother. Her story is unique and could fill the pages of a book itself. I asked her once why she was so difficult as a child. She told me that for seven years she had been the apple of her parents' eyes. Her older brothers and sisters, the eldest being thirteen years older than she, doted on her. When she was growing up, her older sisters, by this time married, bought her presents when they visited. She basked in the attention that she got from the family. Then the youngest son, Wallace, was born and this event changed her little world.

Wallace was born when Mama Moisoff was close to forty-years old. He was the baby, and he was a boy. In many Macedonian-Greek families, boys are everything and daughters are viewed as second-class citizens. This certainly was the case with Wallace. He was everything to them, and as a once favorite child, Libby felt this rejection in a crushing way. This rejection would have a dramatic effect on her life, causing her to seek love and affirmation from a multitude of people. However, once she got through her rebellious youth, she turned this situation into a positive way of looking at life and loving people. Reciprocally, people always responded positively to her.

She never dwelt on negative thoughts. One of my favorite stories of my mother was when she was having a phone conversation with her friend Katie. This friend, somewhat of a morose person, was crying on the phone. My mother asked what was the matter. Katie sobbed, "Oh, I'm so blue and depressed. It's raining outside, and it's dark and gloomy. I just feel like crying. I just don't know what to do. I'm so depressed."

My mother promptly said, "Wait a minute, Katie." She put the phone receiver down and went outside. While out there, she held her hands up to the sky, closed her eyes, and felt the rain as it refreshingly poured on her face and arms. She remained outside for several minutes, coming back into the house quite soaked.

When she picked up the phone receiver, Katie asked, "Where did you go? I've been waiting on the phone a long time."

Mom said, "Well, I was standing outside in the rain."

"Why would you do that?" Katie inquired.

"Well, I wanted to see if it was raining for me and everybody else, too, or just for you. Guess what, Katie—it's raining for all of us, not just you."

I loved that story. It showed that no matter what came her way, she could triumph over it. And much came her way. At age twenty-two, the independent and high-spirited Libby fell in love with a young man named Joe. Six feet tall Joe with piercing blue eyes, reddish-blond hair, and a quick laugh. Joe swept her off her feet. They would go dancing to the Big Band sound in the ballroom at Idora Park in Youngstown, Ohio. They were a stunning couple: Joe with the blue eyes and light hair; Libby a beauty with long, black wavy hair, dark brown eyes, and fair skin. Not only was she beautiful, she was vivacious and could brighten up the room when she walked in. Many of her friends compared her with the then famous starlet, Barbara Stanwyck.

Joe was an interesting man who was born of interesting parentage—ancestry always an important factor in these ethnic families. His gentle mother was born in Austria, and his father was a light haired, blue-eyed Greek from Thessaloniki, Greece. Joe's parents had lived in the United States for many years and had raised a family of two girls and one boy—Joe the oldest and only son in this Greek family. And they did refer to themselves as a Greek family, for it seemed that their German-Austrian heritage lost its identity within the Greek culture of this family. The last name was George, having been shortened from Georgiadis ages ago on Ellis Island in the Port of New York. All three of the George children spoke German, as well as Greek.

Joe loved the Big Band sound, and he loved country music...and he loved Libby. She taught him to play the bass. Not an electric bass, mind you. But a large upright bass that causes blisters to form on your fingers until you develop large calluses, almost as important as skill. She even took him to Mr. Skrbina's home to develop his skill as a bass player. He had a deep, bass voice as well. The two of them were a popular pair at the local dance clubs with many friends as part of their lively circle.

Shortly after their initial meeting, Libby brought Joe home to meet Tate and Mama. Macedonian people, like many ethnic people, can be very super-stitious. No one knows what caused Tate to say this, but when Joe left the room, Tate looked at my mother and said, "Why did you bring home a dead man to marry?" My mother was shocked. In exas-peration she simply yelled, "Tate, what is the matter with you! Why did you say that?"

The incident was forgotten. Joe, who had just returned from military duty in Germany where he served as a translator, as well as a member of the American Military Police (MP's), married my mother. The year was 1950. A good time to celebrate. WW II was over. Yes, there was another war going on—always a war—the Korean Conflict. But it didn't touch their world of new love and happiness.

It was an Orthodox wedding, rich in traditions. In an Orthodox wedding, there are two parts: the Betrothal Service and then the actual Wedding Service. Libby and Joe began the Betrothal Service by standing in front of the *Iconostasis*, the wall at the altar of the church covered with icons. At the *Iconostasis* the priest, dressed in a resplendent black ceremonial robe with gold threads woven into the fabric, took the wedding rings and placed them on their right hands, symbolizing their promise of loyalty and devotion.

The *Kum* or Godfather of the wedding had the privilege of exchanging the rings for the couple illustrating that each partner, both the weaker and the stronger, would complement one another. As Libby leaned her dark head of long, black curls close to Joe's reddish-blonde hair, the couple smiled shyly at one another. Next came the lighting of the candles, which symbolized the five wise maidens of the Bible who had enough oil in their lamps to light the way for the bridegroom—who was Christ. The couple, they were told, likewise, must shine in virtue and purity of good deeds. The climactic moment of the wedding service occurred when Joe and Libby had gold crowns placed on their heads. Wearing these crowns just as regally as any king or queen would, they were led in a procession around the altar in what was called the "Dance of Isaiah." This dance symbolized their first walk as man and wife, and reminded them that they would walk with Christ as their guide. A sweet aroma permeated the ornate Orthodox Church as the priest dispensed incense and a blessing over the couple. To the groom were spoken these words: "Be thou magnificent, O, Bridegroom, as Abraham, the blessed Isaac, and increase as Jacob, walking in peace and working in righteousness and the Commandments of God." The bride's blessing: "And thou, O Bride, be thou magnificent as Sarah, and glad as Rebecca, and do thou increase like Rachel, rejoicing in thine own husband, fulfilling the conditions of the law for it is well pleasing unto God." As the young couple received these blessings, they reverently crossed themselves three times touching their forehead, heart, right shoulder, left shoulder—In the name of the Father, the Son, and the Holy Spirit. Only those with knowledge of the Slavic language understood the wedding vows. Not a word was spoken in English. Nor was the traditional wedding question asked, "Do you take this man, or woman, for better or for worse, in sickness and in health, until death do you part?" These words are never spoken in an Orthodox wedding service since it is believed that the sharing of the Communion or Common Cup, which the couple did, symbolized their agreement to share in times of joy and sorrow. After this lengthy ceremony, the couple exited the church as the choir, in four-part harmony, sang *Mnogaja Ljeta*. The words of the song implored that God would grant them many years.

As the newlyweds, Mr. and Mrs. Joseph George, descended the steep stairs of Holy Trinity Orthodox Church, they were greeted, literally, with dancing in the streets! An orchestra was on hand to *prati* or escort the bride and groom, as the numerous guests encircled the radiant couple and danced a *kolo*, or circle dance. The celebration had begun, and oh, what a celebration! There were massive amounts of ethnic food, continuous live music played by a tamburitzan orchestra, and dancing and singing everywhere.

The couple had borrowed money to pay for the wedding reception themselves. Their parents were not in a financial position to pay for a wedding. Besides, if you paid for one daughter's wedding, then you had to pay for all the others. The ten brides-maids, wearing satin and chiffon gowns that they had worn in other weddings of post-war brides, presented quite a motley blend of blues, greens, pinks, blues, and yellows. None of my mother's friends had money to buy a new dress for this wedding, nor would she have required them to do so.

Barbara and George Raseta were the *Kum* and *Kuma* of the wedding which meant that if any children were born to the bridal couple in the future, the Rasetas would be the godparents, an esteemed position in the Orthodox culture.

The reception came to a close with the traditional bride's dance, or dance of the *nevesta*. A dance circle formed around the bride and guests received a chug of powerful Yugoslavian liquor, *Slivovitza*, as they deposited money into the bridal basket held by the *Kum* and *Kuma* of the wedding. Since Slavic people are known for their generosity, the monetary intake from the bridal dance was quite impressive and gave the new couple a wonderful start. Guests, although struggling with their own economic situation, proudly dropped $20, $50, and even $100 bills into the wedding basket. This impressive sum of money was in addition to the wedding money that had lovingly been placed in envelopes as gifts to the couple. Very few presents such as crystal or linens were bestowed on the wedding couple. Gifts, for the most part, were monetary. The wedding guests, primarily European Americans, had come to bless this new couple and bless them they did! It was a glorious celebration, and Joe and Libby got off to a wonderful and promising life together.

~

The newlyweds settled into a sweet routine and life. At first they lived with Joe's parents, Mary and Arthur George, occupying a little bedroom in the attic where their furniture consisted of a night table and a little bed adorned with a comforter filled with down made from goose feathers. Joe maintained two low paying jobs, one with the Wagner Awning Company and a second job as a truck driver for the Railway Express Company. He started taking classes at Youngstown College, now Youngstown University.

Since Joe spent so many hours working, Libby returned to playing a few musical jobs on the weekends to augment their meager income, as well as to give her something to do—something that she tremendously enjoyed. They treated that music money like little kids receiving a couple of quarters for the candy store. Money from the Awning Company and the Railway Company paid for the bills, or close to it. The music money was for their enjoyment. And life was sweet for them, perhaps a bit poor, but sweet.

A short time after their marriage, they left Joe's boyhood home and purchased a small home of their own on Porter Avenue in Campbell, Ohio, just a few streets up from Mama and Tate Moisoff. After a year of marriage, little Annastasia George was born, always called Stacie Ann, to distinguish her from her namesake, Mama Annastasia Moisoff.

When the nurse brought the newborn baby with a hospital bracelet that read George, Annastasia, to the beaming mother, she joked, "Here's your little Georgie-Porgie, Mrs. George."

Libby, who was absolutely delighted to have a girl, quickly double-checked the gender of her little baby to make sure that she was a girl, and that the nurse hadn't switched babies in the hospital.

From 1950-1952, the couple enjoyed two years of wedded bliss, but this happy time was short-lived. In 1953, tragedy struck. I, little Stacie Ann George, turned two, and celebrated that birthday with a big gathering of family and friends. The family often joked about that birthday party. A tamburitzan orchestra was hired, and the revelers danced and sang to the music, as the succulent aroma of a lamb roasting on a spit, permeated the air. *Nazdravia*—a Slavic toast could be frequently heard as the crowd imbibed on *slivovitza,* that powerful liquor. A myriad of adults attended this celebration of a two-year old child's birthday. In fact, there were few children at this party—mostly the children of relatives—and I, the reason for the celebration, spent much of the evening in my crib. Slavic people could use any small occasion to turn the day into a major celebration. The fact that a child had turned two-years old was only incidental.

It was a good day to celebrate. Just a short time before this date, Joe had been in what seemed like a minor car accident. He was stopped at a railroad crossing when he was hit from behind. Cars were big and sturdy in 1953, and even though the impact caused Joe to bang his head on the steering wheel, it didn't seem to be a major accident. Nothing more was said about the accident.

The month was August. Then the headaches started. Powerful headaches that incapacitated Joe. He would lie for hours on the couch, unable to do anything, barely able to lift up his head. As I romped around near his spot on the couch, he would muster up the energy to joke and say, "This little girl of mine is a beauty. When she gets to high school, if no one takes my little Stacie to the prom, then I'll take her myself." Joe had a brain tumor, complicated by his contraction of meningitis. The technology and expertise in the area of brain tumors and brain surgery in the year 1953 was almost nil.

That was August. At the end of November, he was rushed to the Crile Veteran's Hospital in Cleveland, Ohio, a drive of about an hour and a half from Youngstown. They prepped him for surgery by shaving his head. They didn't even have time to make the first incision. On December 1 at 3:00 A.M., twenty-six year old Joseph George, married three years with a two-year old daughter and a life filled with promise, was pronounced dead. The official death certificate stated in bold, black letters: **brain infection**.

The doctor approached the anxious wife, who would turn twenty-six in five days, and informed her that Mr. Joseph George, her husband, was dead. She looked at the doctor with vacant eyes and kept repeating, "Dead? Dead? What do you mean dead? What about my baby? She's only two? What about her?"

At a loss for any placating answer, the doctor with eyes cast downward and shoulders hunched over, simply walked away.

The next day, as the family was making preparations for Joe's funeral, Joe's faithful dog unexpectedly ran into the street and was killed by a car.

Chapter 11...Raising A Princess

Devojcice Mala   (Young girl)
*Ti si moje srce otrovala   (This is what you did to my
    heart)*

My mother left that hospital a changed and determined woman. One would expect me to say a devastated woman, but that, in appearance, did not seem to be the case. God had granted her a special gift, the ability to take things as they came— good or bad—and to deal with them accordingly. She asked nothing more of life.

In their short time together, the blissful couple never thought to purchase life insurance. I look at that now and I think "How foolish!" But it was 1953. They were young, poor, and in love. How could they have known that Death would pay a visit so soon? There was no money. My twenty-six year old mother went back to work at the bakery where she could earn enough money to pay for my father's funeral and his tombstone. And she did. Having a proper burial is important in ethnic cultures.

What was the visible legacy of a man who had lived a life of twenty-six years? We had those glorious pictures of their wedding, a wristwatch, and his high school ring from East High School, black and gold. Like her mother before her, Libby, in a sense, closed that chapter of her life that dealt with tragedy. Never hearing her own mother talk about the tragedies that overtook her family in Macedonia, Libby, taking that cue, would not talk about this personal tragedy. Her life with Joe was over, and she would not pain herself to think about it anymore. Any information that I was to discover would come later from other relatives. She was determined to move on. Once when I was a little older, she broke that silence and mentioned something poignant about Joe's funeral:

She said, "You know, Stacie, I can't remember who was at my wedding, but I bet I could tell you everyone who was at the funeral." Deep in thought, she started to rattle off a list of names–names of people that I recognized and that had remained close friends with my mother and me for life. She continued her thoughts, "You can always tell who your real friends are when bad times happen. They are the ones who are there for you." I never forgot that truthful adage. Apparently, Mom never forgot that either, making sure that she, as a good friend, was always available for others in times of need.

After my father's death, we sold the little home on Porter Avenue and moved in with my mother's parents, Mama and Tate Moisoff, sharing the same bed that had so recently been my mother's bed as a single woman growing up in that house with the "store front." Even though my father had just died, this was a relatively happy time for me. I recall feeling a sense of loss, but at age two, I was too young to remember my father. Besides, I adored my grandparents. While I basked in their love and the warmth of their household, my mother struggled with what she referred to as "returning to the nest."

We stayed with my grandparents for two years. I was the little princess of the house. My mother's two brothers also lived there: Wallace, part of that once menacing duo and my Uncle Bobby, who had recently divorced and had lost contact with his wife and only son in a bitter custody battle. My uncles treated me as if I were the most precious child that ever walked the face of the earth. Everyone did. You could see it in their faces. I was this little urchin without a father. I was a tiny thing with large, hazel-brown eyes. My uncles would tease me and say if they ever got poor they would put me on the street with a tin, beggar's cup. "With those big, sad eyes," they said, "everyone will be dropping money in the cup. We'll be rich."

They also incessantly teased me about being Greek and told me they were going to send me to Greek school. All the American-Greek children in my community of Campbell, Ohio, went to the public school, as well as Greek language classes (Greek School), and they all spoke Greek fluently. Since I now lived in a house with my Slavic-Macedonian relatives, and not my Greek relatives, I didn't want to be part of the Greek culture at that time and learn the language, something that I greatly regret now.

Uncle Wallace, who had idolized my father, was constantly trying to find ways to make up for my loss. But Uncle Bobby became a surrogate father to me. He filled that big void in my heart, making me feel cared for and absolutely wanted.

In addition to the royal treatment that I received from my uncles, my grandparents spoiled me rotten and took sides with me against my mother. I never knew how hard this must have been for her. But there were many humorous moments.

Once my mother was fixing my hair in the warmest room in that large house, the kitchen. I had long hair, and she would tightly pull it back into a neat ponytail, so tightly, that I often felt that my eyebrows were going up. I started to whine and wiggle as she pulled the rubber band even tighter. Never known for her patience, she smacked me and told me to behave.

My grandfather, always my defender, ran over and yelled at my mother. Her reply:

"Now, Ta, this is my daughter, and this is America. If I want to hit my daughter, I will! This is the American way."

My grandfather drew back his hand, which by this time had become rather useless due to a stroke, and with all the force that he could release, he slapped my mother shouting, "American *vay*, no? She your daughter, no? You can hit her, is American *vay*?? There! Now I hit you. You're my daughter. I proud

American, too! Oh, boy. I like this American *vay!*"

Since none of these blows had actually been struck with much force, and since we were always a family with a sense of humor, we all broke out in laughter, including my heavyset grandmother who had run into the room to see what was going on.

I think my grandparents tried to transfer the love they had withheld from my mother and in some way give it to me. Rather than making amends with her, they sought a reconciliation through me. While it seems so wrong and unfair to her, it was all that they knew how to do. I know that this must have been hard for her. As they held me on a pedestal and praised me for every little thing that I did, they criticized her for everything she did as a mother. Now, mind you, she was not your traditional mother, but we'll save that for later.

~

One day, my grandmother wanted to go downtown and she was going to take me with her. The concept of a mall had not been realized yet. Downtown represented a big shopping district in those days, even in little towns. Youngstown, the nearest major city to Campbell, was neither big nor small–just perfect, as far as we were concerned. I loved going with her to the fish and meat shops where they wrapped your fresh choices in butcher paper. She no longer called the local grocers for delivery. I'm not sure if they had stopped making home deliveries by this time, or if her experience with the "donut conversation" with Mr. Cioffi had been too much for her. My grandmother had favorite bakeries that she visited, and she always bought the same pastries—pastries that today I can't even remember the names, but could still close my eyes and remember the taste and smell.

My grandmother, Baba, as I called her, usually took a bus into town. But my mother, always trying to please her these days, told her that she would drive both of us to town. The following mix-up was bound to happen:

"Mama, where do you want me to pick you and Stacie up?" my mother asked.

"*Vell,* maybe you pick me up McKelvey's," said my Baba.

"OK, McKelvey's, at 4:00," said my mom.

"Oh, no. Never mind McKelvey's. Maybe you pick me up by the cheese store. I need cheese," Baba said.

"OK, you want me to pick you up by the cheese store. You mean the deli?" inquired Mom.

"Yes, deli, that's *vat* I said, you no hear me?" sniffed my grandmother.

Mom responded, "OK, the cheese store, uh, deli, at 4:00, right?"

"*Vell,* no, I think I like McKelvey's better. They have place to sit." Getting frustrated, my mother reiterated the information: "OK. Now Mama, I'm going to pick you up at Mckelvey's at 4:00. Now remember 4:00—McKelvey's. Stacie, don't you forget, McKelvey's. You help your Baba get there."

I sweetly responded, "No I won't forget,

Mommy. McKelvey's at 4:00." Four o'clock came, and my mother promptly pulled in front of McKelvey's department store. She was concerned for her mother who was overweight, a diabetic, and who tired easily. No sign of Stacie. No sign of Baba. My mother drove back to the "cheese store." No sign of Baba at the deli. No sign of Stacie. She frantically drove up and down the streets of downtown Youngstown. She tried the other major department store, Strouss. She searched at the Five and Dime store, Woolworth's. No sign of her mother or her daughter. Then after one last attempt, she discovered her missing passengers. There on an obscure little side street was a pouting little Stacie and a furious and out of breath Mama. My mother quickly pulled the car up said, "Mama, you said that you would be at McKelvey's."

My grandmother angrily responded, "No, no, no, I didn't say *dat*! I said I *vould* be at the bakery. I *alvays* go to the bakery last. You know I love *dat* bakery. You *neverr* listen to me."

Siding with my grandmother as usual I replied, "That's right Baba, you told Mommy the bakery. I heard you."

An angry Baba got into the car. The atmosphere was chock full of intensity and bad feelings. But it wasn't over yet. We headed home to Campbell from Youngstown, just a few miles away. Typically, Ohio communities are incredibly flat. But Campbell, Ohio, close to the border of Western Pennsylvania has a few steep hills.

My mother, most of her young adult life, has had

cars that never worked properly. This car was no exception. As we approached the top of the hill, my grandmother realized that she had forgotten something, and she wanted to quickly go back to town.

As my mother turned the car around and started to go down the steep hill, she realized that her brakes weren't working! Not wanting to cause a panic, she maintained an even-toned voice and started pumping the brake. As it became obvious that something was wrong, she calmly told her mother and daughter, "Now I don't want the two of you to worry, but my brakes aren't working. I'm going to try to move this car to the side of the road, and it may be a bit bumpy, so hold on." Now the expected response from my grandmother should have been one of worry or hysterics, but instead she answered, "Oh, *surrre* (rolling her r's more than usual) for your friends you have brakes. For Dorothy Galida you have brakes. For Renee Jamrozik you have brakes, but for your mother you *neverr* have brakes! *Nista!* (Nothing!)

And I, the little urchin, echoed, "Yeaaaa, Mommy, for Baba you never have brakes! *Nista!*" That was the last time my mother drove us downtown. For her remaining years, Baba always used public transportation to go downtown, and everybody was happy.

Chapter 12...Building a Home

Floodwaters rising
Meshing into rich, Ohio soil
Neighbors scrambling for higher ground
A young man misses the mark
Falling head first into swelling waters
It's everyman for himself
All but one ignore his pleas
Forfeiting his high ground of safety
He plunges into the watery abyss
Diving, diving, diving
He tries to save
The vortex is encompassing
All is darkness and water
Two mothers weep

My mother was not a typical woman of the '50s, or '60s, or any era for that matter. An independent spirit and a woman ahead of her time, she called her own shots. Never the Harriet Nelson type, she hated fitting into the mold of what women should be or should do. And now, she had her fill of living with her parents. There never was an incident or a time that she ever verbally complained. But she was twenty-eight years old now with a four-year old daughter, and she wanted a place of her own with that daughter. We were always a pair. I may have sided with my over-indulgent grandparents, but we were always a pair, Stacie and Libby, wherever we went.

She purchased a corner property on the top of Penhale Avenue and 15th street, one street over and two streets up from her parents' home. The ground was composed of that black, Ohio dirt richly fertilized from years of cows pasturing on that hill. She organized a group of her male, carpenter friends and her brothers, and as she donned a shovel herself, work on our home began.

The footer of that home had just been completed when tragedy struck. Two years after the death of my young father, Death would once again snatch one of our young men. This time it was Uncle Bobby.

My Uncle Bobby, now divorced, had become my surrogate father. I adored him. He was handsome, musically talented, and possessed a great sense of humor, as did all the Moisoff children. I remember playing a game with him where he would let me sit on his chest and he would pretend to be screaming in agony as I pulled the hairs off his chest. I don't think I actually was ever strong enough to truly pull the hairs but the situation, strangely enough, was always hilarious to me! Then he would sing to me and create lyrics to songs with great sound effects just as his father—my grandfather—did. If he sang a song about drinking a soda, he would make the sound effects of a bottle opening and splashing out. Every song and every word became a vivid picture in my mind. I truly enjoyed the colorful, musical element of my family.

It was a summer afternoon, and we all needed a break from the work on the home. My mother and I decided to go on an outing to Mill Creek Park, a quaint park with a once active flour mill, a creek, and an abundance of trees. There are a few incidents that I distinctly remember about that day, even though I was only a child of four: One was that we observed a group of Native Americans recreating a "rain dance" in the park. This had great significance to me because it, indeed, began to rain. Not just a gentle rain; it was a deluge! Within minutes, this downpour sent dozens of picnickers in the park scurrying for shelter. The second distinct memory I have of that afternoon was my mother and I running into a ladies' room at Mill Creek Park for temporary shelter. While hovering in the corner of that crowded restroom, I can recall hearing music coming from somewhere, playing Patty Page singing the *Tennessee Waltz*. Since we were a musical family, we were very aware of the background music in stores, restaurants, and other public places. Even at four, I was attentive to background music.

The rain and storm became stronger. I wasn't afraid. I was never afraid when I was with my mother. She was strong, and she could conquer anything, as far as I was concerned. And I recognized that she would do anything for me and my safety. There are things that day that passed in a blur.

It poured like never before, causing flooding in the
streets. This normally would not have happened, but
the gutters and sewers in our town of Campbell, for
some reason, were clogged. In a matter of a few
minutes, the town experienced the devastation of a
flash flood. The damage to the town was immense,
but for us, the flood had a personal devastation.

My Uncle Bobby was at a local business estab-
lishment in the community, located at the bottom of
the hill. As he surveyed the rising water from the
vantage point of a porch, he saw an unoccupied car
spinning in the murky, swirling water. Closely
following the vehicle was a man bobbing up and
down, screaming for help. The man was Steve
Paulin, my Uncle Bobby's friend, who had jumped
into the water to try to stop what apparently was his
car. My uncle, I am told, without any thought of the
consequences, jumped into the raging waters to try
to save that man's life. Both young men were caught
in the vortex of that flood. The car, covered in four
feet of raging, muddy water, pinned both men down.
Two other men, Steve O'Dea and Glazar Dimoff,
watching in horror, tried to grab Uncle Bobby and
Steve Paulin, but their efforts only caused them to
almost be sucked into the current. Men on the side of
the road formed a human chain and rescued Steve
O'Dea and Glazar Dimoff. But Bobby, who had
valiantly tried to save Steve Paulin, had been pinned
down underneath the water too long, and tragically,
both Bobby and Steve Paulin drowned that horrible
day in 1956. My precious Uncle Bobby and Mr.
Paulin, both young men, lost their lives in the only

major flood to occur in the history of the city of Campbell, Ohio, located high on a hill. Ironically, the police officer on duty, Officer Masi, who was my Uncle Bobby's good friend and had spent ma~ evenings eating dinner at Mama Moisoff's ' was the bearer of the bad tidings.

"Hello, Mrs. Moisoff," Officer softly.

"Oh, Hello. *Sedi.* Sit dov̶ ͜ᴜst made some pork chops. This i͛ ͬ͜r *ve* having. I be nervous for my ᶠ ͬ͜ot home. I *vait-ing* for Bobby tͬ ͜ͻ eat. He be late. Go ahead—eat ͷe come soon," Mama sweetly

" ͤ don't know how to tell you this. ͜ ͟ ͜ nave to." He began to sob. "Bobby ͜g home. He drowned today in this horri- ͜ᴜd."

A thud was heard. Mama Moisoff upon hearing the news fainted before anyone could catch her. The Red Cross had actively been working in the community due to the nature of the flood, and some of the workers were called to come to the Moisoff home.

The magnitude of the flood was so great, that people got into makeshift boats to come over to the house. Later, an attorney visited my grandfather.

"Mr. Moisoff. I believe that I have some good news for you. I think that you can get some compensation...well, some money from the city of Campbell for the death of your son." There was no response from my grandfather. The attorney continued, "Yes, you see, Mr. Moisoff, this tragedy did not have to happen. The sewers were clogged, thus causing the waters to rise at an exceptional level— and they rose much too quickly. That was the city's fault. The city, well, the powers that be of this city—they are responsible for this disaster. Your son did not have to die like this, and therefore, you should be eligible for some money, perhaps a good bit of money."

My grandfather's nostrils flared. He spat on the kitchen floor and looked squarely in the eyes of the attorney.

"Money? *Vill* that bring back my son? No! You keep your filthy dirty money. Just give me back my son."

Macedonians know how to mourn. And they know how to wail. When my mother and I arrived at my grandparents' home that dreadful day, having rushed home from Mill Creek Park once the waters had subsided to some extent, the women led by my grandmother were wailing. Sensing that something was dreadfully wrong, but not really wanting to know the truth, I timidly asked my *Dedo,* my grandfather, "Where's Uncle Bobby?"

With tears in his eyes, and puffing on his ever-present cigarette, he replied, "He went to Florida."

The funeral was awful. In those days and in that ethnic culture, children went to funerals, even if they were four years old. I remember my grandmother wailing and screaming and being held back from the grave as she tried to throw her body into the open grave. The Orthodox choir sang the traditional funeral song, a dirge, *Vecnija Panja.* Having heard this song so many times before, I curiously asked one of the relatives what it meant.

"It means that the person in the coffin has fallen. Yes, he has fallen. And indeed, he *is* dead," she replied, placing special emphasis on the IS DEAD part. Literally, the dirge was part of the Orthodox liturgy beseeching God to have mercy on the soul of the departed. But the explanation given to me as a child sufficed: He is fallen and he is dead. As I thought about the meaning of the words, a silly thought came to my child's mind. At Easter morning service, the priest always proclaimed, "*Christos vos Krese*! Christ is risen!" And the congregation responded, "*Voistinu Vos Krese*! Truly He is risen!" I thought of my Uncle Bobby in that coffin, and said to myself, "Uncle Bobby is dead! He is dead, truly!"

The mournful notes of this dirge, sung in a minor key with four part harmony, seemed to re-enforce the wailing of the women at the funeral. Funerals, at this time, included watching the coffin being lowered into the ground, and the mourners throwing handfuls of dirt on to the coffin. The sound of dirt and pebbles clanking on the metal coffin was spine-chilling to me. My Aunt Annette, after the dirt had covered the coffin, poured coffee over the grave. I'm not sure if this was a religious tradition, or if my *Tete* (Aunt) Annette, who was very dramatic, simply did this. Tete Annette had dearly loved her brother Bobby, and Bobby had loved his coffee. Her gesture of pouring coffee over his grave, in her mind, was an act of love. She would continue to do this at his grave for many years, which only made her older sister Stella very upset. Stella was a no-nonsense type of woman who hated funerals so much that she absolutely refused to attend a funeral service. Even years later when her own mother died, she would not attend the funeral service. Besides that, she hated anything that she thought was too dramatic, particularly if it related to a Macedonian custom or tradition. Since just about everything we did as a family was dramatic, this created some tension.

~

In the short span of two years, both of my grandmothers had lost their sons, snuffed out in the prime of their lives. At the time of his death, my father was 26; Uncle Bobby died at age 36. Even though I was only four at the time, it struck me how differently the two mothers dealt with the deaths of their sons. My father's mother, Mary George, who truly grieved, stated, "The Lord giveth and the Lord taketh. Blessed be the name of the Lord." Baba George never grew bitter, never asked why, and praised God until the day she died.

Baba Moisoff was another matter. As long as I live, the memory of my grandmother throwing all of her clothing into a large, old-fashioned wringer washer filled with black and deep purple Rit dye will be indelibly etched in my mind. After that dreadful day, followed by the horrific funeral service, Annastasia Stojanoff Moisoff, who mentally and emotionally had survived the brutal butchering of her parents by the Turks in the Old Country, would never regain her health. Wearing the dyed black and purple clothes, she spent the remaining years of her life in mourning. Her surviving children repeatedly reassured her that they were there for her—that she had grandchildren and many family members to live for. She didn't seem to care. She would never walk into a church again without wailing, screaming, or fainting. I, who always hated these episodes and dreaded the times when she would come to church, was mildly surprised when I realized the people of our parish, Holy Trinity Orthodox Church, seemed to take this ritual and display of emotion as a normal reaction. Perhaps to them it was the proper way to express grief, showing honor and respect for the deceased. Maybe I was becoming *Americanized*, like Uncles Walter and Donald, like Aunt Louise. Later in life, I tried to make some sense, maybe for my own comfort, of my uncle's death. My only thought came from the Bible, "Greater love has no one than this, that he lay down his life for his friends." John 15: 13

It always gave me great comfort that my beloved uncle had given his life trying to save another man. My family was made of noble stuff.

Chapter 13...
Living the Single Life

Ne placi moja ljubavi (Don't cry my love)

The back to back deaths in our family caused great personal changes. "Back to back deaths." What a horrid expression; what a horrid reality. So much better to be talking about something else—like back to back Superbowl championships or back to back movie blockbusters. But our legacy was back to back deaths. The changes within family members varied. Mama Moisoff, never recovered; Tate Moisoff lost much of his zeal for life. Uncle Wallace got a tattoo with his brother's name, Boris, on the forearm. My mother, a strong swimmer, became afraid of water after the drowning death of her brother. And me—I became prayerful, almost to the point of hysteria. Each morning I uttered the same prayer, "Dear God, please don't let anyone else in my family die today, especially my mommy. Amen."

In spite of the tragedies, it wasn't in my mother's nature to pine away. As her thirtieth birthday approached, and she had endured almost four years of mourning, she came to a realization that she was too young to remain the shattered widow forever. Life in recent years had been too sad; it was time to have fun now. The fact that she had a little daughter was absolutely no hindrance to her at all. Her child would just go along—dates and all.

Initially, Mom's return to the social scene involved group activities connected with the Serbian Orthodox Church. Even though our nationality was Macedonian, as Orthodox Slavs, we felt quite at home worshiping at the Serbian Orthodox Church; besides, there wasn't a Macedonian Orthodox Church in the area at that time since many of the Macedonian immigrants had moved from Youngstown to the Akron-Cleveland, Ohio area. Those friends from my grandfather's village of Prilep were long gone.

We attended choir concerts, basketball tournaments, and music festivals. To experience these events was to witness a European subculture within the American culture.

Once our church, Holy Trinity Serbian Orthodox Church of Youngstown, Ohio, hosted a choir festival with choirs from all over the area including the special guest choir from Lackawanna, New York. Choir members had arrived by train on the P & LE Railroad (Pittsburgh and Lake Erie) and were housed in the homes of the Youngstown parish members, including our home, the one that my mother had built on Penhale Avenue, now completed. After a weekend of dancing, singing, and bonding, it was time to say goodbye to our guests from Lackawanna. The congregation went to the railroad station to *prati* the departing guests—to send them off with tamburitzan music and singing. As I stood on the platform of the railroad station and waved to the moving locomotive, I realized that my mother, one of the musicians, was still on the train bound for Lackawanna, New York! I started yelling at the top of my voice for the train to stop. So did everyone else. With a loud whistle, the train about fifty yards down the track, made a sudden stop and out came a smiling Mom, tambura and all! The crowd cheered! I don't ever recall the P & LE Railroad company making such an abrupt stop in a non-designated area!

~

Then came the actual dates with men. Dating was great, and it was always a threesome—Mom, the date, and me. Happy to be with her, I never questioned why she had me tag along on those dates.

My mother's beaux, and there were many, tended to be classically good-looking men, always Slavic in background: Macedonians, Croatians, and Serbians her preferred types, although an Italian showed up for a few dates. The Slavic men and my mother had a connection with their second language-Slavic, their love for tamburitzan music, and of course, they had to show some love and affection for her little daughter. I think that this was the main reason that she dragged me along on her dates; it was a test. She knew that the guys liked her, but what about her little girl?

There was one suitor that particularly struck my fancy—Eddie. Smelling strongly of Old Spice cologne and always chewing wads of Juicy Fruit gum, Eddie was a favorite of mine. With his dark, black moustache that curled slightly at the edges and thick, black eyebrows to match, he bore a slight resemblance to the then popular actor Tyrone Power. Since Mom resembled the actress Barbara Stanwyck, especially with her dark eyes and long, black curls, the pair turned heads wherever they went. Typically our dates—and I do say *ours* because it never occurred to me that I was a third party—were treks to Idora Park, an enchanting amusement park in Youngstown, Ohio. I would spend what seemed liked hours in the magical world of Kiddie Land as the handsome pair smiled and waved incessantly to me at each ride. Eddie must have truly been smitten with my mother for him to spend all that time waving ecstatically to a little girl whose greatest feat was riding in a circle on a brightly painted turtle. I never seemed to have enough of those rides, but finally, they would coerce me off the rides, and we would enjoy the famous Idora Park french fries. Today, amusement parks everywhere offer freshly cut potatoes fried to perfection. They give these potato eateries clever names like the Potato Patch, or Spuds Aplenty and such, but in 1957, this little treat was a novelty and the rage at Idora Park. The french fries were huge, and we would smother them with vinegar and ketchup. On the way home we would solidify the makings of an upset stomach by munching on caramel apples and cotton candy. In my mother's attempt to combine dating and child rearing, she managed to add to the spoiled nature of her little girl. This became apparent when after one such wonderful outing, feeling that my riding time had not been sufficient, I looked at my mother and defiantly said, "I hate you. I hope you die." Considering the frequent deaths of young people in our family, this had an incredibly devastating punch to it. The three of us looked at each other—all shocked by my words, including me. It was the sweet-smelling, gum chewing Eddie who broke the silence: "Stacie Ann, you know you don't mean that, honey. Say you are sorry to your mother."

I don't remember responding to his request, but I know that after that incident, my "dating days" dramatically stopped. I wasn't a bad child, only precocious and quite spoiled. How could it be otherwise? In the family's attempt to shower me with love to compensate for the loss of my father, as well as my beloved uncle, they overdid it. Their greatest flaw was too much love for me.

So things changed at this point. What should have been a punishment for my rude behavior actually precipitated the most wonderful times of my young life. For the next two years, as my mother did her dating without me, I was shuttled back and forth among four wonderful people: my maternal grandparents Annastasia and Dimko Moisoff, and Mary and Arthur George, the parents of my dead father. While regretting my loss of dating status, I embarked on two years of magical times with my two grandmothers whom I called *Baba George* and *Baba Moisoff,* and my two grandfathers, whom I called *Dedo George* and *Dedo Moisoff.*

At the home of the Georges, I was able to piece together a portrait of my father, their beloved son, who had walked so briefly on this earth. The saying goes that "Only the good die young," and after listening to stories about him, I certainly believed this to be true. Years later I would meet acquaintances and distant relatives of my father and they would say, "Your father was the nicest man. He would do anything for anybody. And he had such a wonderful laugh and sense of humor."

Many years later, one relative said in a most flattering way, "I loved your father. He was such a sweet man, and you've grown up just like him." I especially appreciated this comment because it came from one of my cousins, Vicki Drumm Stefanov, who knew first hand what a precocious child I had been. I believe that she was absolutely relieved that I had turned out just as I did, and her worst fears concerning me had not come to fruition.

Many relatives would tell me, "Your father loved your mother so much. It was a marriage made in heaven."

While at my grandparents' home, I received a great heirloom from them: a musical recording of my father. A few years before his death, my father had been at a local amusement park where they permitted you to make a recording on what was called a 45 RPM. For a few bucks, my father made a recording that became one of our most treasured keepsakes of him. The recording began with an explanation:

"This is Joe George singing a little bit of Vaughn Monroe to Libby." In a deep, bass voice he began to sing a cappella:

I'll see you in my dreams, Hold you in my dreams
Someone took you out of my arms, Still I feel the
thrill of your charms
Lips that once were mine, Tender eyes that shine
They will light my way tonight
I'll see you in my dreams.

Not remembering the man himself, the resonating sound of my father's voice on the recording always startles me. The deepness of his voice seems to contrast with the gentle, twinkling blue eyes in one of the few photographs that I have of him. I loved this photo from 1951, not processed in Kodak color, but in a colorized brownish hue which accentuated his reddish, dark blonde hair and the impeccably tailored brown suit that he is wearing, tailored in his own father's shop.

The pale blueness of his eyes seems to jump out in this sea of brown. His smile is captivating, and somehow, it just makes you want to know this man. Regrettably, I never will. Hearing his voice and his love song to my mother triggers a stabbing pain from deep within my heart, but I'm so grateful for this precious keepsake of this man, my father. I've heard this said by others, and I know this to be true myself: When a child loses a parent early in life, that void is always there. A child spends a lifetime looking and trying to fill that void, and asking why, and wondering what could have been. The loss never completely goes away, although the Lord in his infinite mercy would provide others in my life to ease that pain and fill my wounded heart with love.

So my mental portrait of my father, drawn from the stories of many relatives and friends, was a very positive one. My mother broke her silence on one occasion and described one of their dates to me. They had gone to the movies, but on their way to the theater, they had an argument. My mother was furious and in her anger, refused to sit with him in the movie theater. As she sat close to the front of the screen, and he sat in the back of the theater, she could hear him roaring with laughter throughout the opening cartoons, shown routinely before the featured presentation in those days. She couldn't believe that he could still manage to laugh at a cartoon after they had such a heated argument. His laughter was infectious, and she found herself laughing, too, so she got up and joined him at his seat in the back of the theater. The couple promptly made up.

"You just can't stay mad at a grown man who laughs his heart out watching a *Tom and Jerry* cartoon," she said with a little twinkle in her eye.

In addition to feeding my hunger for stories about my father, my paternal grandparents, of German and Greek heritage, fed my stomach with

Greek staples such as feta cheese, black Greek olives, succulent lamb, and Greek butter cookies called *kourabiethes,* but more importantly, my gentle grandmother, Mary, fed my soul.

Chapter 14...
Taking Care of Others

"For I was hungry and you gave me something to eat,
I was thirsty and you gave me something to drink,
I was a stranger and you invited me in,
I needed clothes and you clothed me,
I was sick and you looked after me...
Whatsoever you do for the least of my brothers,
That you do unto me."
Matthew 25:35-40

In a relatively short selection entitled *Where Love Is, God Is*, the Russian author Leo Tolstoy presents a beautiful tale of a cobbler, Martin Avdeich, who is searching for God. In this Russian short story, God tells Martin to look out of his shop's window for He (God) will be there.

As the story progresses, Martin desperately looks out the window of his cobbler's shop searching for a glimpse of God. Instead of seeing God, he has three encounters: one with a Russian soldier, chilled to the bone by the cold Russian winter; a poor young woman with a hungry babe in her arms; finally, he meets a disgruntled old woman. While awaiting this visible manifestation of God, Martin ministers to the needs of these wretched Russian peasants. This includes providing food, shelter, warmth, and compassion. Growing impatient with God's lack of an appearance, Martin cries out to God, "Where are you? You said that you would visit me today!"

God replies to Martin: "Martin, when you provided the cloak for the freezing old soldier, I was there. When you fed the impoverished soldier's wife and her baby, I was there. When you gave words of peace and comfort to the old woman, I was there. Yes, Martin, it was I."

How do we test our love for God? The answer to that test, some have said, is to love others.

Perhaps this is the most precious legacy of my grandmothers. Through their love for others, they gave me a glimpse of God. Many people talk about their religion, and they talk about God. Through these willing vessels, my grandmothers, I was able to see God's love in action. While Annastasia Moisoff, the most generous of people, showed me how to be charitable, it was my father's mother, Mary Gaps George, a German woman, born in a little village called Elok Srem in Austria, who gave me my first lessons about Christ's love.

Mary's German heritage somehow got lost in her marriage to a Greek man, but if her cultural heritage blended with his Greek heritage, her religion stayed strong. She was a Roman Catholic, but religion and God were much more than a denomination to her. Religion and a love of God represented life itself. Any thought or action she took was prefaced by the saying, "Lord willing."

Mary Gaps George was born in Austria in 1906 with a minor eye deformity, one that would have been easily remedied at birth had she been born in the United States, or at a later time in history. In fact, close to her 74th birthday, she did have it surgically corrected. Her left eyelid closed sleepily over the eye causing her to give the impression that she was winking at you. To her family, it was an endearing face to behold; yet she reminisced of childhood times when school children made fun of her. Nevertheless, closed eye and all, she managed to capture the heart of the handsome Arthur George. She always referred to him as her "honey," and he called her *Marika*, the Greek form of Mary. She remained a devoted wife, faithfully caring for him even later in life when he became terminally ill.

They met when she was nineteen and he, 34. A big age difference, a bigger cultural difference. He was a highly educated man from Thessoloniki, Greece, recognized at the university for his proficiency in several languages. When he came through Ellis Island, his credentials and his last name were lost to him. As he received permission to enter the great land of opportunity that was America, the inspector wrote his name as Arthur George, rather than Arthur Georgiadis, his true name. His university credentials from Greece had no validity in the

States, so without any regrets or misgivings, he pursued another career, that of a tailor. He managed to open his own shop, and one of the first workers that he hired was a young, German girl of nineteen, Mary Gaps, who soon became his bride.

Mary was a gentle woman with a servant's heart. Not only did she care for her husband until his death, she faithfully took care of her mother, Eva Gaps, until her mother died at age 90.

There was an immense contrast between the gentleness of Mary Gaps George and her grumpy, sour-faced mother whom I always referred to as German Grandma Gaps. Even though the Gaps family was born in Elok Srem, Austria, they always considered themselves to be Germans. Maybe it was great grandmother's ramrod straight posture that reminded me of a German soldier (This was about ten years after World War II had ended, and the war stories still abounded, as did my imagination), or maybe it was her curt, harsh treatment of my beloved grandmother. Whatever the reason, I was always afraid of her. My most vivid memory of German Grandma Gaps was of her looking disparagingly at me, chin slightly raised, her hooked nose a little pinched as she questioned partially in German and partially in English, "*Vas is dis?*" The meaning of that three-word phrase was "What are you doing?" I may have been precocious, but I was always well-behaved. Spending so much time in a world of adults, I acted like an adult in a little body, so I am not sure what I did that annoyed her so much. Maybe she was just annoyed about life.

But my Grandmother Mary taught me about sacrificial love for others, and in her love for others, I was able to capture a vision of Christ. Through her actions, and not merely words, she reflected Christ. No matter how she was treated by others, including a stern mother, she always responded in love. She was a Roman Catholic, and I was being raised Eastern Orthodox, but she never tried to convert me. She didn't need to; our connection wasn't a church denomination—it was Jesus Christ and His great love. I believe the roots of my adult faith were grounded those many years ago in a little white house on the east side of Youngstown, Ohio— grounded and firmly set by the gentlest of women. Even as she herself suffered and mourned the death of her only son, she would humbly say, "The Lord given, and the Lord taketh, blessed be the name of the Lord."

Chapter 15...
Whetting the Musical Appetite

Pile moje malo   (My little one)
Zasto mi places ti? (Why are you crying?)

When a child loses a parent at age two, the potential for any negative psychological developments is great. This could have been the case, and perhaps, should have been the case. But through God's great mercy, the love and enrichment I shared with not only my mother, but the four grandparents, as well as numerous aunts, uncles, and cousins, counteracted, I believe, any negative psychological developments that could have occurred in my young life.

It is stated in the Bible that the steps of a righteous man are ordered by God. It is His divine plan that sets us on our course, and hopefully, we follow his direction and guidance in pursuing that course. But life's experiences and special moments sometimes set in motion the particulars and details of that course. Just as my Grandmother Mary laid a firm foundation of faith in my young mind, my maternal grandfather, Dimko Moisoff, would whet my appetite with the gift of music.

It began with a mandolin. In 2001, Nicholas Cage and Penelope Cruz starred in a movie entitled *Captain Corelli's Mandolin*, based on a book by Louis de Bernieres. In this movie, Captain Corelli, an Italian soldier as well as a musician, packed his mandolin on his back and entered war-torn Cephalonia, Greece. In somewhat of a plot reversal, my grandfather packed his mandolin on his back and left war-torn Macedonia for the safe shores of America. Dimko began his musical career in the United States playing in a band consisting of a guitarist, a clarinetist, a bass, and my grandfather on mandolin. Sometimes they would hire a percussionist to give them an extra beat for their musical sound. They played in the local cafes, for church picnics, dances (called *vecerinkas*), and other activities. The lyrics of their songs often expressed their love of the Old Country, a very incongruous theme; for most of the men hated the Old Country and never wanted to go back. They were perfectly happy in America.

By the time I came along, Grandfather Dimko, *Dedo*, with his right arm now paralyzed from a stroke, had long quit playing in the cafes. His daughter Libby now continued that tradition. But it was I, her daughter, who sat at Dedo Moisoff's feet and spent hour upon hour listening to his stories and his music. His songs were versatile: sometimes war songs, sometimes love ballads. As an instructor of poetry teaches his students the technique of onomatopoeia, my grandfather would use special sound effects to give emphasis to the words he sang. For instance, whenever he sang a war song about the Turks and the Macedonians, he literally would spew out the word TURK, and in doing so, he gave me a glimpse of the hatred still shared by those two ethnic groups at that particular time in history. But most of the time, the songs that he taught me were loving and playful.

Since I adored my grandfather and everything that he did, I was fascinated, just as my mother had been a generation earlier, with that beautiful mandolin of his. Inlaid with mother-of-pearl around the edges and a beautiful inlaid mother-of-pearl butterfly inset, it was quite a treasure. I would try to play it, but my fingers were so small that whenever I tried to depress the frets, the sound would always stay the same. Besides, its belly-back shape made it impossible for me to hold it on my tiny lap. My grandfather, sitting patiently, would proudly clap and shout, "Bravo! Bravo! Play it again! *Jos Jedan!*" Somehow he made me believe that I could play this instrument—and play it I would! I had music in my blood, heart, and soul—and there would be no turning back. From that young age until, well—forever, I would play stringed-instruments, my preferred instrument being the *prim*, a mandolin-sounding instrument of the tamburitzan family.

The prim was the lead instrument in the tamburitzan orchestra and it played the melody line, or the harmony line if there were two prims in the orchestra. High pitched and sounding like a mandolin, it always reminded me of my grandfather. Music was our passion—a very important part of our lives. But there were other fond memories that I shared with my grandparents.

~

I turned five and began making many preparations for that big stepping stone in life...kindergarten. The school, Penhale Avenue Elementary, was about four blocks from my grandparents' home and about seven blocks from my own home. The family decided that Dedo would walk me home from kindergarten every day. I would arrive at his home where my mother would be waiting for me to drive me to our own house.

The big day came. Dressed in a crisp, navy blue and white dress, accented by my black Mary Jane shoes and white-laced socks, I, in a state of excitement, went to school.

Every child manages to tuck away a memory or two concerning his or her big first day in kindergarten, but for me, two episodes stand out in my mind: The first episode involved that well-conceived plan to have my grandfather walk me home from school to his house on Devitt Avenue where my mother would pick me up. But when she arrived, we weren't back. She couldn't imagine what was taking us so long; the school wasn't that far from their home. She pathetically looked at her mother for some encouraging news as to the whereabouts of this twosome. Baba Moisoff, eagerly awaiting our return and preparing an after school snack of cheeses, fresh fruits, green peppers, and bread, nervously shook her head in a negative response. Most families would probably remain calm in a situation like this, but our family with its history of tragedies tended to immediately move into panic mode first and sorted out the details later. My mother was true to form: she was bordering on hysteria. She went outside and frantically began asking neighbors if they had seen her father or me. Relatively soon, a friendly neighbor approached her with some information:

"Phil," my mother asked, "Did you see my father and Stacie? I can't find them anywhere! They were supposed to be home a long time ago."

Phil calmly replied, "Oh, yeah, Libby, I saw them on Hyatt Avenue—three streets over."

"Hyatt? What are they doing over there?" asked my mother. "That's not even on the way home!"

"Well," said Phil, "The last I saw them, your seventy-some year old father was jumping and hopping over cracks in the sidewalk. They were doing this all around the streets of Campbell. People are passing them, smiling, blowing their horns at them, and waving."

"What are you talking about, Phil?" my mother impatiently asked, "Why would my father, at his age, hop and jump around the sidewalks in Campbell?"

"Well, Libby, I said to your father, 'Mr. Moisoff,

what on earth are you and your granddaughter, Stacie, doing?'"

"What did he say?" my mother impatiently asked, and Phil, doing his best imitation of my grandfather replied, *"Vell,* Phillip, you see, my Stacie told me that if I step on a crack, I *vill brreak* my mother's back, so you see, *ve* hopping over all the cracks so *ve* don't do *dat!*"

My mother, who by this time had achieved some local celebrity status in the community through her music and radio show, responded in dismay, "Do you mean to tell me, Phil, that my father has been walking all over this city and avoiding the cracks in the sidewalk just because of some silly little girl's game?"

"Yep! That's about the size of it," said the smiling Phil. My mother was flabbergasted! But for me, this event was magical. Imagine having a grandfather like that—a grandfather that encouraged you to be the most colorful, dramatic, and creative person that you could possibly be! A grandfather that allowed your imagination to soar to the highest places. Nothing was too silly or unattainable.

~

To be sure, my mother was not to be undone in her colorful personality. Thus, we have the second episode of Day One of my kindergarten experience: The teacher, Miss Vargo, who was Mom's former high school classmate, told each of the kindergarten boys and girls to have their mothers sew their names on the inside of their sweaters or jackets for identification. It was 1956—women sewed, and they sewed frequently. I came home that afternoon, having completed my sidewalk jumping and crack-avoiding walk with my grandfather, and proudly informed my mother of the mandate given by the all-powerful kindergarten teacher, Miss Vargo. She truly was a sweet woman, but at this stage in my life, she loomed large and mighty, and to me, her word was THE WORD.

"Mommy, Teacher says you have to sew my name on to my clothes for tomorrow." There, I had regally stated the command. Now my mother must obey.

My mother casually inquired, "Are all the other mothers sewing the names on the backs of their coats and sweaters of their kids?"

"Yes, Mommy, teacher said you have to do this," I, the consummate rule-follower stated.

My mother who could wield a hammer with the best of men, but hated sewing responded: "Well, you tell your teacher that if all the kids have their names sewn on in their clothes, then yours will be the one that isn't sewn—and you will always know which one is yours."

Needing desperately to fit in, I didn't think that this was too funny, but my teacher Miss Vargo and all her colleagues that she told, thought this concept was hilarious. And the most astonishing thing to me at that time was that I never did get my coat or sweater confused with anyone else's in the class that entire year!

Chapter 16...Marrying Again

With this ring
I thee wed

By the time that I turned six, Mom and I had settled into a peaceful routine. On weekends she dated or went with her friends, and I stayed with my grandparents, but during the week, I lived with her in the house that she had built. Since my mother had been widowed at such a young age, she prudently had this house designed into two large apartments, not merely a duplex, for it was too massive to be classified as such. Instead, the structure of its design resembled two houses within one house, and we comfortably lived in the downstairs apartment/house. Her idea was that she could always have renters if things got difficult for her financially.

Before the need to supplement her income occurred, her single status changed. One night **he** just appeared at our home. Even at age six, I recognized that he was unlike the other men that she had dated.

His name was Casimir John Fill—not the typical
Balkan name, or type of man that sauntered through
our doors. No, **he** wasn't your Steve, or Milan, or
Dusan type with an "ich" or "off " at the ending of
his name designating his Balkan heritage. He wasn't
like the other suitors in temperament, either. They
were musicians, partygoers—free spirits just like my
mother. No, he was not like the others; he was more
sedate and a good bit older than she. After a brief
courting, they hopped in a car with two of their
friends as witnesses and headed to New York to be
married in one of the worst snow storms of the
decade. It was Valentine's Day. I was six-years old
and not sure how I felt about this; no one had asked
me. In a most remarkable gesture, however, this man
not only asked my mother's parents if he could marry
their daughter, he also asked the parents of my dead
father if he could marry their former daughter-in-law.
As he visited the Georges' house, his words were
extraordinary: "Mr. and Mrs. George, I would like to
marry your daughter-in-law, and I promise that I will
take care of her and your little granddaughter Stacie.
You don't have to worry." What an incredible man of
honor! But it would take a while before my child's
mind and heart could appreciate the goodness and
virtue of this man.

Now it was the three of us living in the house on
Penhale Avenue that my mother had built, one street
over from her parents. As the years passed, I would
grow to love this man who was steady as a rock, and
indeed, I would call him my father—for he became
that to me. But struggling to remain what I thought

was loyal to my dead father, I resisted accepting him during those early months of their marriage. More comically, I disliked his name, Cas John Fill. I thought the name had a ridiculous sound to it. Since I refused to call him "Daddy" in those early months, I precociously called him "John." This was most outrageous since this was merely a middle name. At school I would fill out forms and in the blank where it asked for the father's name, I would dramatically write in bold letters, DEAD. There was a place for guardian, and I neatly wrote John Fill. At one point the school called our home asking who exactly was John Fill?

One day he gently asked me to put my toys away and in true, evil stepchild fashion, I put my little hand on my hip and said, "I don't have to listen to you; you're not my father." I had stung him. Good. Yes, that's what I wanted to do. I saw him, for a brief second, wince with pain—as if he had been stabbed. Suddenly I wasn't so proud of what I had done. He never said a word. Out of his hearing, it was one of my mother's sisters who reprimanded me. I adored my mom's sisters and her brothers, and their advice had great import to me.

I listened intently as my beloved Tete Annette said, "Honey, you can't do that. He's your father now, and he loves you. He's going to take care of you. So you have to love him back and call him Daddy. You be a good girl now, Stacie."

"Wow!" I thought. "These were my mom's people. If they thought that it was OK to love him, well, then maybe it was OK."

Timidly at first, I started calling him Daddy. He acted as though this was the most natural thing in the world for me to do. This was good. Had he responded otherwise, I would have been so humiliated. But he didn't. In the years that followed, he became my defender, protector, confidant, and yes, my father. Once someone came up to him and said, "I saw your stepdaughter in a concert. She was good."

He coldly answered the man, "That is not my stepdaughter—that's my daughter, and yes, she was good." He never officially adopted me. In a feeble attempt to keep the memory of Joseph George alive, the promise was made to my paternal grandparents and my mother that I would keep the last name George until I married. Whether or not this was a wise decision, it didn't matter. I always cherished the memory of my dead father, but I embraced Cas John Fill as my father and the man who raised me.

As I went through my school years and performed in numerous musical concerts, he became my most ardent fan, cheerfully sitting through every vocal and instrumental recital, including my accordion recitals—an event that would try the patience of the most supportive parent. I would scan the audience to see where he was sitting. When our eyes met, he would respond one of two ways: He either would form his fingers to make the sign for "OK," or he would shake his head for no. The gestures weren't given in response to my performance; to him, I was always good. The OK sign meant that the volume was good; the negative shaking of his head meant that he couldn't hear me. That's the only thing that concerned him—whether I was loud enough. My Cousin Sandy, one of the singers in the all-girl orchestra that we would form when I was a young teen once said, "Your father stayed in the background to be our audience so that we could be up front. He stayed in the background so we could shine in the spotlight."

In the years that I had the privilege of calling him my father, I learned geography through his very vivid descriptions of such places as the Aleutian Islands, where he had proudly served our country in World War II. Each month he received his issue of *National Geographic* magazine, my Christmas gift to him, and we would share the stories and wonderful adventures that those places represented. Years later, I would always choose him to be on my team when the family played *Trivial Pursuit*. With his knowledge of geography and world events, you couldn't lose if you were on his team. While my mother always moved at a fast pace, his style was slow and steady. He always had time to stop and admire the beautiful world around him. From a very early age, I could identify various trees because of his training.

"Look there, Stace," he would say. "You see that beautiful tree over there? That's a pin oak. It starts out small and slow, but when it's done growing, it's beautiful." Always pronouncing the word *beautiful* as *bee a u ti ful*, he enabled me to visualize this lovely, full-grown tree.

He, also, made me proud to be an American. I always found it interesting that my family with such strong roots in the Old Country had such a love for

America. I saw the evidence of that with my grand-parents and that was true for my stepfather. In one breath he would speak fluent Polish, and in the next breath, recount the minute details of the Battle of Gettysburg, or some minor American military conflict that most people had no clue that it had existed.

In Deuteronomy 5:16, the Lord commands, "Honor your father and your mother, as the Lord your God has commanded you, so that you may live long and that it may go well with you in the land your God is giving you." I always focused on the part that said "so that you may live long." But, truly, the blessing of honoring your father and mother wasn't about long life, but the fulfillment of the second part of that verse, "that it may go well with you in the land your God is giving you." My dad chose to love me; I chose to honor him. It went well for both of us!

Chapter 17...
Swimming and Sinking

Ne plac mala (Don't cry little one)

Like many children of musical parents, I liked to be on center stage. Typically, that stage involved music, dancing, or drama. But this time, it was through athletics that I gave my mother another opportunity to sit in the audience and applaud. I never was, nor never will be classified as an athlete. But there was one thing that I could do quite well athletically speaking, and that was to swim.

In the late 1950s, the city of Youngstown boasted of both a YWCA and a YMCA which offered many activities for children, so my mom enrolled me in the winter program at the local YWCA which met every Saturday. My morning sessions involved ceramics, which was OK, but in the afternoon, I joyfully took swimming lessons in a beautiful, indoor, Olympic-sized pool. Basking in the success of my swimming lessons, I thoroughly enjoyed my time spent at the Y. The instructors placed me in the advanced swimming class, and since I was quite young, this thrilled me. The family joked and said that I was part fish since I loved the water so much.

The notice went out: PARENTS NIGHT. The time had come to show off the many swimming skills that we had learned. The parents were seated in the bleachers behind a high guard rail that encircled the pool. My mother was my only relative in the bleachers that day, and I proudly smiled at her as I took my place in line. The swimming instructor nodded to me. My task was to dive into the water, swim to the middle of the pool to a "fireman's pole." When I reached the pole, the goal was to shimmy down the pole in the water, come up, and return back to the starting point. I'm not sure the point of this exercise, but I had completed it dozens of times and was quite adept at the task.

Standing on the diving board in my navy blue tank suit and white bathing cap, I prepared to dive. Suddenly I froze. The probability of reaching that pole, I reasoned, was nil. Was the instructor crazy? The pole looked miles away! I started to panic. The swimming coach sternly yelled, "You can do it, Stacie! Dive!" I started to cry. "I said dive!" was her stern admonishment. A rule-follower by habit, I responded to her command and plopped myself into the pool, but I didn't take a breath before diving. When I hit the water, I panicked and started to bob up and down yelling, "Help! Help! I'm drowning!"

The coach responded, "No, you're not! You can do it!" "NO! NO! I can't! Help! Help!" I gasped taking in large gulps of water.

My mother sitting in the bleachers with dozens of other parents took one look at my face and saw fear. Without hesitating, she heroically jumped over the high guard rail, grabbed the lifeguard's pole and extended it to me. When it didn't quite reach, she jumped into the water—clothes and all—and yanked me out, like the catch of the day!

I gratefully held on as my mother, my heroine, placed me on dry land, and in my mind, saved me from the clutches of death! I was sent back to the dressing room where the swimming coach prepared to give my mother a lecture on meddling. She was mistaken. It would not be my mother who received the lecture.

"Mrs. Fill, that scene was uncalled for. Your daughter was capable of swimming and executing her skill," said the coach. "You prevented her from completing her task."

"You must be the most heartless person that I ever saw," retorted my mother. "My little girl was going under. I saw the look in her eyes and that look was fear and nobody, not even you with your coach's badge, was going to stop me from saving my little girl!"

For the next two weeks, I inhaled antibiotics to treat the bladder infection that I had contracted from consuming too much pool water. But I had a smile on my face. I had witnessed a great life lesson being played out: Never mess with Mama Bear!

~

My mother's philosophy and teaching of "not messing with Mama Bear" would resurface later in my life. It occurred many years after the diving incident. By this time, I was a young woman of twenty involved in teaching a dancing class to a group of junior high school boys and girls. One of the boys was very athletic. In fact, he played basketball and baseball for his junior high school teams. But a dancer he was not. Every week his mother brought him to these lessons and faithfully paid his weekly fee for the class. I found his inability to follow dancing instructions quite frustrating. Moreover, I felt that they were wasting their money.

"The boy wants to play basketball, not dance," I said to some friends. "I am going to tell his mother that she is wasting her money on these lessons. This will be for his own good. Look at the expression on his face while he's taking his dance class— it's one of sheer agony."

I thought that I was so smart. I was in control of the situation and I was going to do this family a favor.

The next day, with a great sense of self-importance, I approached the boy's mother and very emphatically informed her of the following: "Your son just isn't a dancer. I think that you are wasting your money and you should seriously consider withdrawing him from lessons." There, I had stated the facts and now the mother, I was certain, would respond with swift action to my suggestion. Swift was the response, but totally unexpected. The mother was furious with me and responded with a tirade of insults. I was shocked! Looking for support from my own mother, I called her and told her what had happened. Mom listened intently and then once again taught me the lesson about Mama Bear.

"You know, Stacie, that boy was that woman's only son and to her, and to any mother for that matter, their child is the best. She was really proud of him, even though you didn't think that he had any talent. You shouldn't have said those things to her."

"What do you mean?" I angrily responded. "I said those things for that boy's own good! I was saving her money! I thought that you would understand!"

"It doesn't matter what you thought. When you attack the cub, you are messing with Mama Bear, and honey, you never want to do that!"

She was right. As I pursued a career as a schoolteacher in the years to come and had children of my own, I never forgot those words. They have served me well when I've chosen to use them; when I haven't, the results have been disastrous. The adage is a trustworthy saying: **NEVER MESS WITH MAMA BEAR!**

Chapter 18...Having A Baby

Zibala Majka zibicu   (My dear mother)
Pjevala ti, O pjesmicu   (Sing me the songs)
Spavaj, spavaj, angel moj   (Sleep, sleep, my angel)
Ti si bio moj   (You are mine)

The 1960s have been labeled by some as "the decade that changed the world." In those years we, as a nation, mourned the brutal assassinations of President John Fitzgerald Kennedy, his brother Robert Kennedy, and Dr. Martin Luther King, Jr. The South staggered with racial strife, and the birth pangs of a most unpopular conflict, Vietnam, surfaced. But for me, an event much closer to home would change my life: the birth of my only sibling.

A precocious eight-year old by now, I longed for the companionship of a brother, or sister. I often would dream that I had a brother, and I even gave him a name and a face. I called him Joe, and I had great plans for him. Now it was going to happen: my mother was going to have a baby. The reality that an actual baby, boy or girl, was on its way was beyond anything that I could imagine! Some "only children" anticipate the birth of a sibling with fear and jealousy, recognizing that life as they know it will change drastically. This was not my reaction. I rejoiced, as did my stepfather. He was now thirty-seven years old, and even though we had truly bonded as father and daughter, a child of his own at this somewhat "late" age for fatherhood was a most, pleasing thought to him.

Months before the birth of this most awaited baby, Mom, Dad, and I went on a family vacation to the nation's capital, Washington, D.C. My dad, a World War II veteran and a profound lover of American history, proudly narrated our family's tour of the Capitol, the Washington Monument, the Lincoln Memorial, and other significant landmarks of Washington. Thoroughly tired, I slept peacefully in the back seat of the car as we headed home, northwest to Ohio. As we approached an intersection, my sleep was abruptly halted as I was thrown to the floor of the car. We had been hit from behind by a driver who had fallen asleep at the wheel. It wasn't a significant accident, practically a fender bender. The accident would not have been cause for worry except for one fact: my mother was several months pregnant, and she had taken quite a jolt from the accident. As I lifted my head and shaken body from the floor of the backseat, I could hear her crying. To make matters worse, the driver was a soldier on furlough in the Washington area. He was devastated that he had caused this accident. My father, always the proud, military man, tried to comfort the young soldier. After everyone calmed down and Mom had received medical attention, we continued our journey home valiantly attempting to put the event behind us. It wouldn't go away. A few weeks later, my only sibling, a baby girl, arrived in this world prematurely. Had she been born at a later time in history, the knowledge and excellence of neo-natal care would have allowed her to thrive physically and mentally. But it was October 1959, and my precious new sister was born with brain damage which would worsen as she grew older. At that early stage in her life, we weren't even aware of the extent of the brain damage.

Named Sally (*Sava* in Slavic) after one of my mother's best friends, the baby grew, but each step of her development was painstakingly slow and laborious, whether it was taking her first step, being weaned from a bottle, or being potty trained. It was especially trying for my mother who always did everything at a fast pace. Sally's child rearing demanded patience, often to the point of frustration. Patience was not something that my mother possessed, but my stepfather moved at a slower pace—just the right pace for Sally. This daughter, born to him when he was close to forty-years old, was the world to him and the two of them would have one of the closest and sweetest relationships that ever existed between father and daughter. To him, she was perfect. And, indeed, in God's eyes she was.

The year would continue to ravage my mother. After weeks in the hospital, our little "preemie" came home. But before she set foot in her new home on

Penhale Avenue, the baby was presented to her maternal grandparents. My mother, so involved in the premature birth of her baby, didn't realize how sick her own mother, Annastasia, had become. When presented with her new granddaughter, Baba Moisoff seemed shocked and confused. My mother, accustomed to the loving nature of her own mother, especially where babies were concerned, was puzzled by this reaction. What we didn't know was that Baba Moisoff, a diabetic, had quit taking her insulin shots. She was sixty-four years old, and having lost her beloved son Bobby four years earlier, she simply felt that life was too burdensome for her. His death had taken away her joy and will to live. The family often reminded her that she had other children, but it was to no avail. After Bobby's tragic death from drowning, her heart was broken. As a Christian woman, she would never contemplate suicide; she simply wouldn't give life any help. Withdrawal from her insulin seemed like an effective plan and regrettably, it was. She was rushed by ambulance to the hospital where she remained in a coma for several weeks. It was December 25, Christmas Day, and she seemed to be getting better. With all of the family at the hospital, my mother decided to send me and my dad to his mother's house to celebrate Christmas with his family. This "step" family of mine had embraced me with all the love that any family could give, and I felt truly blessed. Not only did I have grandparents, aunts, uncles, and cousins on my mother's and father's side, but on my stepfather's side as well. His large family showered me with affection—and lots and lots of presents! The situation was quite pleasing to me. In this family, I was one of nine grandchildren and the oldest. I felt quite important with the pecking order.

As we cousins played in the center of a room filled with adult relatives, the phone rang. Why the very first ring of that phone sounded ominous to my little ears, I don't know, but it did. One of the aunts answered it, paused, and then hung up the receiver. She looked at me with great pity and said, "Stacie, honey, your grandmother, your Baba Moisoff, well, uh, she went to be with Jesus." With all eyes on me, I began to dance around the room in a rather hysterical fashion. I remember looking down at my shiny, black Mary Jane shoes, white-laced socks trimmed with embroidered red roses, and my crisp, black and white taffeta Christmas dress. I started humming and dancing around in a circle. Then I suddenly collapsed on the floor and sobbed my little heart out. My beloved grandmother, Annastasia Moisoff, after whom I was named, was gone.

Chapter 19...
Healing and Recovering

He has sent me to bind up the brokenhearted,
To proclaim freedom for the captives,
And release from darkness for the prisoners.
Isaiah 61: 1

Where there is great joy in life, great sadness often lurks in the shadows. Our family seemed to receive double portions of both. The response to these significant moments in our lives would test our mettle. The writer Rudyard Kipling labeled triumph and disaster as imposters and said to treat them both the same. The family, now recovering from a third death in a short period of time, had to come to grips with life and the conditions it presented. Once again, each of us would respond differently. For my mother, it was probably her darkest time. With each death of a family member, a small piece of her strength was chipped away. She managed to rise up from the ashes of widowhood, only to lose her beloved brother. Now experiencing post-partum blues, heightened by the birth of a handicapped child, the loss of her precious mother was staggering. What many family members never realized was that she, of all the siblings, was the daughter who had to go to the morgue to identify the drowned body of her brother. Now once again, with the assistance of a dear friend from the Serbian Orthodox Church, she was required to go to the funeral home to make all the arrangements for the burial of her mother.

She began to have severe nightmares. One night, thrashing from one of these horrific nightmares, she shoved her hand through a window. Awakened by the sounds of shattering glass, I witnessed the incident. It was devastating to me. My mother, the strength and pillar of my life, was struggling, and I didn't know what to do. As my sense of serenity and well-being ebbed, I started to have nightmares myself. I was prone to constant crying and my once happy demeanor was sullen. My mother, even in her suffering, recognized that I needed help. A typical reaction to this situation would be to seek professional help. However, that wasn't the course of action that my mother chose. While she, personally, seemed to lose some of her faith in God at this time, she recognized my great need for a great comforter. Our neighbors, the Siraks, had a little altar in their home. This was the remedy that my mother thought that I needed. She called our neighbors and told them that I was coming over, and she sent me out the door—by myself. I nervously knocked on the neighbor's door and that sweet neighbor woman, Mrs. Sirak, let me in, acting as if this were an everyday occurrence. She brought me to the little altar that had a statue of Mary. I looked at it apprehensively, for even then, something in my little mind told me that it was just a statue, and it didn't hold any power to comfort me. Mrs. Sirak leaned down and asked me if I wanted to pray to Mary. I said no. But I closed my eyes, and while Mrs. Sirak stood over me, her long, brown hair touching the tip of my head, I uttered these words: "Jesus, please help me. Please help my mommy. Amen." That little prayer of nine words had life-changing results. As I said the amen, I could feel this heaviness lifting from my heart. In the Gospel of Mark, Jesus says, "Let the little children come to me and do not hinder them, for the kingdom of God belongs to such as these."

This little child caught a glimpse of heaven that day. I left the Sirak's home a joyful child once again. My mother recovered from this difficult time. But the most precious gift I received from that day was that I knew right then and there that I had an advocate in my life. I realized that there would never be a moment, nor any circumstance that I would face alone. I had a Great Comforter—a Great Healer in Jesus. That lesson would never leave me and would serve as the anchor of my life.

Very shortly, I would need to draw on the peace that the Comforter brings. About a year after the death of my grandmother, a tragic event involving my childhood friend, Monica Pacak, occurred. Our friendship began with music lessons.

Since my family was quite musical, particularly with stringed instruments including guitars and the tamburitzan instruments, they assumed that I would want to play these instruments. It never occurred to them that I wouldn't want to play the tambura. The question that they asked me was, "Stacie, besides playing the tambura, what <u>other</u> instrument would you like to play?"

At age six, I started playing the tambura, first under the tutelage of my beloved grandfather, then in an orchestra with intense musical instruction. My mother purchased two handcrafted instruments called *prims*: one was for me and the other instrument, identical to mine, was for my girlfriend Monica Pacak. Monica's parents and my parents had been friends for a long time and each summer our families would join four other families from Campbell, Ohio, and we vacationed together. After selecting a vacation spot that promised plenty of swimming, fishing, and boating, the families would rent cottages located in a row with paths connecting one cottage to the other. Sometimes they would rent a large house or two and the families would share those houses. While the parents had maintained friendships since grammar school days, we children developed friendships simply because we were thrown together. The five oldest children, Mariann Hudak, Ricky Jamrozik, Janice Strollo, Monica Pacak, and I had very different personalities and roles to play within the group.

In addition to vacationing together, Mariann, Monica, and I all participated in Mr. Pete Zugcic's

Children's Tamburitzan Orchestra. Monica and I sat together in the first row during orchestra practice. There really wasn't a "first chair" concept in this children's tamburitzan orchestra, but we, nevertheless, played the "lead" instruments. The identical instruments that my mother had purchased for us weren't crafted by the hands of a master craftsman, as my later instruments would be. These instruments were crafted with children in mind: durability was a must. Beginning tamburitzan players struggled with learning to control the movement of the wrist. It took many years before the goal was reached: a clear sounding *tremolo* that was achieved by learning to control the pick while rapidly hitting the strings. Beginner's instruments often displayed multiple scratch marks etched into the fine, cherry wood surrounding the sound hole of the tamburitzan instrument, unlike the instruments of skilled tamburitzan musicians who deftly picked at the strings without ever making a mark. We children labored to attain this goal. In the early days of my musical training, I left the music class often frustrated from my inability to produce a clear tone. My fingers were too tiny to depress the strings enough to make different notes, so every note sounded the same. My tremolo was sloppy and certainly not anywhere near the rapid speed that was required. But I practiced and practiced, until finally, I discovered that I had earned those desired calluses on the fingers of my left hand—those calluses so needed to provide a clear sounding musical note. I began to play music, and it was thrilling to me.

My friend Monica and I enjoyed playing music together in the orchestra. Our instructor would give us new sheet music every week: waltzes, polkas, ballads, Slavic folk tunes. Each week we faithfully came to music practice and became more proficient in our musical task. We never wasted time for small talk. We simply sat down in our designated seats and played music, week after week. And then one week that seemed just like any other, Monica didn't come to orchestra practice. Another week went by, and Monica was absent again. Almost without any warning, she got sick, very sick, and just as suddenly, she died. Monica had a rare blood disease, something that was incomprehensible to me as a child. I was only nine years old; so was she.   I remember walking into the funeral home and thinking that I certainly spent a great deal of time in this ugly place. I nervously stood at the back of the room, and my mother told me that I had to walk down to see Monica. I was shaking with fear and didn't want to walk down to the coffin that held that little body. I had witnessed so many deaths by this time. But this was different. She was young, and she was my friend. We played music together; we even had identical instruments. How could she be dead?

As I started to walk towards the little coffin, my heart started beating rapidly. In my vivid imagination, I thought that I saw Monica's chest going up and down. "Was she breathing? Why do they have her in that coffin if she's still breathing?" I wanted to scream and bolt out of that awful place. My mother told me to touch Monica's hands and say good by to her. This, to my mother, wasn't really that odd. It was part of the culture. People would go up to the coffin of a dead person and touch their hands, or even kiss them on the cheek or on their hands as a sign of great love and respect. I hated this and couldn't understand why she would want me to do this. I glanced over to where her stricken mother and father sat, their eyes swollen from crying. Just as I was ready to run out, someone in the room, I don't remember who it was, gently placed her hands on my shoulders and tenderly said, "Doesn't she look pretty? In my mind's eye, I remembered Monica with the blond hair and blue eyes. But these eyes were now tightly closed, and I didn't think that there was anything pretty about a dead little nine-year old, who was my orchestra friend. But I was too upset to respond, too upset to even cry, so I politely shook my head in an affirmative gesture. Someone hugged me and reminded me that Monica and I were such good friends. It could have been Monica's mother, Mrs. Pacak, whom we all called Jay Jay.

My family and the Pacak family remained close friends over the years following Monica's death, and I witnessed something extraordinary in Jay Jay. Having lost her beautiful little girl, nothing in life could ever hurt her as much as this loss. We, as a family, had lost young ones and we could share in Jay Jay Pacak's pain. But it was time for us to heal and move forward. Life was about living, not only dying.

Libby's Tamburitzans prepare to perform at President Jimmy Carter's Inaugural Ball. Center: Libby Fill; Back row: Stacie Vesolich, Darlene Balog Fejka, and Steve Vesolich.

Libby and Joseph George on their wedding day.

Lt. to rt. Uncle Gligor, Uncle Walter,
Mama Moisoff, Sandy, Tete Annette, Nettie,
and Tate Moisoff.

Rising of the
Next Generation
Part II

Chapter 20...Crossing Borders

Vesela Sestra (Happy Sisters)
Nam srce dira (Touch my heart)

With his beloved Annastasia gone, Dimko didn't last too much longer—two years, to be exact. He stayed in his own home for awhile, but really wasn't able to take care of himself. I would often visit him after school and he, trying to imitate my grandmother's incredible gift of hospitality, would offer me cookies, or other food items. Not wanting to embarrass my grandfather, I painstakingly swallowed the food items that were stale and sometimes rancid. It was time for Dedo Moisoff to move in to one of the homes of his children. This is what our people did; they took care of their aged parents. A nursing home was not an option.

My mother immediately made preparations for her father to live with us, assuming that he would want to remain a resident of Campbell, Ohio. Having built the home on Penhale Avenue into two large apartments, she had rented the upstairs apartment to a lovely couple named Louise and Pappy. Not only were they wonderful tenants, but they had become good friends with our family. She had rented this apartment after she married my stepfather, deciding that we really didn't need to live in the whole house. Now it pained her to inform Louise and Pappy that they had to move. She nervously approached them, "I've got some news that may upset you, Louise. You will have to move out because my father is too sick to live alone. He needs to move in with us very soon."

Upon hearing the news, Louise sobbed. This experience was so distasteful to Louise and her husband, that they chose to build their own home after they moved out of the apartment, vowing never to rent again for fear of being asked by a landlord to abruptly leave their home.

After all the preparations were made, and the couple had reluctantly moved out, Dedo gave us a surprise. Offering no explanation, he simply and firmly stated that he would not move in with his daughter Libby and live in the house on Penhale Avenue. For the longest time, he fought the need to move in with any of his children until he got extremely ill, and he was forced to move in with Tete (Aunt) Annette in Akron. While I am sure that my mother was pleased with the care that her father was receiving from her older sister, she was hurt that he had not chosen to live with her. His time with Tete Annette and her family was brief. At age 76, Dimko Moisoff, my mother's Tate and my

Dedo, died, leaving his family saddened and ending a significant connection with the "Old Country." His children and their children would have to hold the torch and perpetuate his and Annastasia's legacy. The two of them had left a meager amount of money in insurance policies to their five surviving children and numerous grandchildren and great-grandchildren. The estate consisted of the sale of their modest house and property—which they sold to a church—and the distribution of their furniture to family members. The most precious heirloom, his mandolin, was given to the eldest daughter Stella, an accomplished mandolin player herself. When she was in her mid-seventies, my Tete Stella gave the mandolin to me to keep for my son Stephen until he was older. Tete Stella felt that this was appropriate since both Stephen and I played guitars and mandolins.

"Stacie, at the end of his life, your Dedo was too sick to think straight and give you this mandolin," she informed me. "I know that he would have wanted you to have this since you have played music all your life, and your Dedo loved you so much. But rather than just give it to you, I want to give it to my great-nephew Stephen since he plays stringed instruments. This way, the music will go on for generations to come." No sum of money could have equaled the value of that gift to Stephen and to me.

After Dedo's death, the family unit seemed to disintegrate at first. Uncle Wallace, my mother's youngest brother moved to San Francisco with his family, never to return East. If we wanted to see him and his three children, we had to fly to California. But after a time of mourning and healing, the family re-grouped, drawing closer to one another. My mother's other remaining brother, Eli or *Be eell*, Southern style, remained in Richmond, Virginia, with his family who journeyed north every fall for a visit. Uncle Eli and his wife, Aunt Louise, loved the picturesque, Ohio Indian summers and autumn foliage. To return the gesture, every summer the "northern family" or "The Yankees" as we were called by our Southern cousins traveled to Virginia to visit with Uncle Eli and his family. This included our family of four, my Tete Annette's family of four, and Tete Stella and Uncle Donald. Frequently, the married children of Tete Stella and Uncle Donald— Donnie and Vicki and their families—joined us. The relatives stayed at my uncle's spacious home, thus inviting both fond memories as well as the chaos that can occur with so many people vacationing under one roof. In those days, no one ever considered making reservations at a hotel. The children, mostly all young teens by now, stayed in the finished basement which, for the most part, was off-limits to the adults. We loved our freedom. The cousins, at least seven of us, were all two years apart which made for some great camaraderie. My sister Sally, eight years younger than I and mentally handicapped, sadly, was often excluded from this special time with the cousins and spent most of her hours with my stepfather who kindly gave my mother uninterrupted time with her sisters and brother.

After their parents died, the three sisters did

everything together, and to be with them was a great adventure. We nicknamed them the Three *Sestras* (sisters) and joked that they were like the three *cabaleros* of Spanish folk song fame. One summer, instead of going to Richmond, we decided to trek to Canada to attend a Macedonian dance called a *vecerinka*. A live Macedonian band consisting of trumpets, clarinets, accordions, and mandolins would provide hours and hours of music for our dancing pleasure. After packing ample supplies of feta cheese, hard salami sandwiches, fresh fruit, and *zelnic*, that Macedonian pastry of spinach and feta cheese wrapped in phyllo dough, the family piled into a large station wagon.

For this trip we took the three sisters, four of the cousins, and our great aunt, Tete Maritza, who had a thick Macedonian accent. Being the youngest, my cousin Nettie and I were forced to sit in the "caboose" of the station wagon, riding backwards. This was risky business since I always managed to get carsick, but fortunately, I was fine for this trip. It was a wonderful trip. The sisters always sang in three-part harmonies, and we cousins joined them. In addition to the old Macedonian favorites, the car resounded with the sounds of *Sentimental Journey, The Old Rugged Cross, Won't You Come Home Bill Bailey, Lay My Burdens Down by The Riverside, and Your Cheatin' Heart,* just to name a few of their very eclectic favorites. To be in the midst of that loving group was pure delight, and all went well until the return trip home when we attempted to re-enter the United States.

As we crossed the Canadian-USA border, we were stopped by a friendly border patrol. Doing his job, the young man asked the question by rote, "Are you all American citizens?" The question was simple enough and one that we all could have answered with an unequivocal "Yes." However, we had forgotten about Tete Maritza. She had become a naturalized American citizen a few years before, but naturalized or not, nothing would hide that thick, Macedonian accent. Proud of her American citizenship, Tete Maritza, of all the members in the car, decided to respond to his routine question. In the thickest accent possible, she leaned her dark head out the window of the car and proudly replied, *"Ya, I Amerrrrrican ceeteezen* (with special emphasis on her rolled r's.) *I cum to theese cuntree long time ago. I be verrry verrry prroud Amerrrrrican citeezen!"*

With remarkable efficiency, the border patrol motioned us to pull our station wagon over to the checkpoint where we were detained for several hours clearing up our identities and American citizenship. The biggest reason that it took so long was that the three *sestras* couldn't stop laughing. Having lost his smile, the once friendly border patrol didn't see the humor of the situation. As he grew more upset, Tete Maritza kept talking and talking to him, which only made matters worse—and the "Three Sestras" just kept laughing. Laughter, music, and drama-always the main ingredients of our outings!

~

On one trip, we headed to New York City. By this time our family was in the birthing stage of forming a band and pursuing a musical career, but the musicians and singers at this early stage had not been organized. Instead, our "band" was a reluctant family trio consisting of my mother playing her guitar-sounding instrument called a *bugarija*, my cousin Sandy with her incredible voice and beauty, and me—barely thirteen and very unhappy about this band concept. In this band, I played my *prim,* that mandolin-sounding instrument that I had learned from both my grandfather and years of lessons in the youth tamburitzan orchestras. Thinking like a true musician, Mom recognized that New York was the place to be if we wanted to break into national fame with our ethnic music. She put her plans into motion by combining a family vacation with a musical venture. In addition to our little trio, Tete Annette and her other daughter Nettie would travel with us. We meticulously packed our instruments, safeguarding those precious items from heat damage. But instead of packing our traditional performance attire, the sedate black skirts with pretty white tops and black vests, Mom had bolder plans. In the bottom of her suitcase neatly folded, lay four black skirts, four black satin blouses, four canary yellow vests with tomato red fringe, and four red sashes. As I entered the room, I heard her grumbling: "How on earth am I going to pack these four hats?"

"Mom," I nervously asked looking at the four sombreros that matched perfectly with the canary yellow vests, "why are you packing these yellow and red clothes?"

"These are our costumes, when we go to New York," she responded with confidence.

"Costumes? Costumes? What do you mean by costumes?" I began to sweat. I thought of my junior high school friends. What would they think? What if someone took a picture of us in those hideous outfits! I thought of me, the junior high school girl, desperately trying to maintain my image of a fashionably dressed, popular teen. Image, of course, was everything in junior high school. Braces on my teeth, skinny legs, and flat chested—all these elements had already undermined my image. I didn't require additional help from Mom. Yet, I knew that I could not change her plans. If Mom said we would wear these clothes, we would, without a doubt, wear these clothes. But they would not be worn without some resistance!

She continued with what I perceived as a horror story. "You know, New York has a large Spanish population. Spanish people like guitar music. If they see us in these costumes, they will relate to our music. They'll think that we're a mariachi band." I glared at her. She calmly responded to my glare, "Don't look at me like that. You always worry about everything."

New York City had a large Spanish population. Yes. That was one of the few points that we could agree on during this so called family trip. I couldn't believe that I had to wear that hideous costume.

"I can't wear that outfit! It's ridiculous! These costumes don't look Spanish— they just look

stupid!" I ranted and raved and kept making a clicking sound with my tongue as it touched the roof of
my mouth. The sound was for emphasis and definitely communicated my annoyance with the idea of
wearing these outlandish costumes.

"Don't *tsuts* at me!" Mom bellowed in response
to the clicking sound that actually did sound like *tsuts.*

Always trying to act intelligent, I arrogantly
snapped, "There's no such word as *tsuts* in the
English language."

"Listen, Miss Know-It-All, I just made a new
word-*tsuts*!" she responded. "Never mind about
these costumes. We'll look like a band. Just shut up
and wear them." When Mom was in what I called
her "band leader" mode, she was formidable.

For me, the costumes were not the worst part of
our musical venture to New York City. Mom had
neglected to arrange for any musical bookings for
our trip. Having read far too many magazines on
how celebrities had been discovered, Mom naively
believed that we could travel to New York, play in
the hotel lobby, and *voila*, they would discover this
unique family band! All of my years growing up, I
struggled to be like everyone else, or at least what I
thought represented everyone else. *Everyone else*, I
just knew, was reserved and refined, never drawing
attention to themselves. Just ordinary people doing
ordinary things, but not my family. God had placed
me smack dab in the middle of a family that did
everything with great flare and somehow managed
to *always* draw attention to themselves. When they
entered a room, everyone knew that they had

arrived. Ordinary people doing ordinary things? Never! Not my family—they were anything, but ordinary. This trip to New York fit right into the normal scheme of *un*ordinary things. So in the lobby of that hotel, to this day I've blocked out the memory of the name of the hotel, we sang and we played our hearts out. Well, at least some members of this family band did. Sandy, now in high school and always comfortable and graceful in any situation, enjoyed herself. Mom, likewise, was having the time of her life. I, on the other hand, wanted to blend into the flowered wall paper. I kept my eyes downcast and my lips frozen in a grimace.

"She could make me play," I grunted, "but she can't force me to smile."

Our "gig" in the lobby did not lead to our discovery. Redemption was near, however. In New York City lived one of our Macedonian-American cousins, Jordan Christopher, who had attained some celebrity for two reasons: First, he prospered as a musician in the city, but more importantly, he had married Sybil Burton, ex-wife of actor Richard Burton. When Jordan and Sybil got married, we had attended their wedding reception and had met both Sybil and her daughter Kate, who was Richard Burton's daughter. Our family, raised in a tiny, Ohio suburb, was star struck. At this particular moment in time, Cousin Jordan served as my knight in shining armor by rescuing me, a damsel in distress, from that hotel lobby! After receiving our phone call, he promptly arrived in a black limousine. We stood frozen in our tracks gazing at the magnificent vehicle, obviously something that we had never experienced. Ordering us to get in, we were chauffeured to Cousin Jordan's swank, New York City restaurant where we received the royal treatment. Cousin Jordan proudly introduced us, his family, to his circle of jet-set friends.

"Slavic people always take care of their own," Mom commented and abruptly decided that we didn't really need to play music any more in New York. We would enjoy the sights, which we did, seeing for the first time the Statue of Liberty—that significant landmark in the life of my Grandmother Annastasia. After enjoying our time as tourists, we headed back to Ohio. Our polished sound and lucrative career as musicians would come later. As we left New York City, I breathed a great big sigh of relief. It would be many years before I returned.

Chapter 21...
Taming the Gypsy Spirit

Evo banke, cigane moj , (Here my gypsy)
Cigane moj, sviraj me ti! (My gypsy, play for me!)

Tate Moisoff always referred to his daughter Libby as a gypsy. He would tell her, not always in a pleasant manner, "You know in Old Country there be hundreds of *vomen* like you—even *yourr vun tete* (aunt) be like you. You get *borred,* you get restless, you—how do you say— you pick up and go. You *neverr* tell nobody *verre* you go. You gypsy *voman*!"

It was true. Libby, although born and bred in America by a traditional mother, was like these women. Her spirit simply got restless, and she had to go somewhere. Through her very persuasive nature, she coaxed friends to go with her at the drop of a hat. But if they weren't able to go with her, she had no fear of traveling alone. She simply got in her van and drove off, leaving no word with anyone where she was, or where she was going. Sometimes she went to Geneva on the Lake, a favorite tourist attraction on Lake Erie. Other times she went where she could hear music, preferably tamburitzan music. More often than not, she just dropped in a friend or relative's house and stayed overnight. She never called to tell them that she was coming, yet they all seemed to be thrilled, actually honored, that she had graced them with her presence. If she hadn't adequately packed her bag with amenities such as toothpaste, soap, or even a nightgown, since sometimes she just took off without even planning on staying overnight, her hostess gladly supplied her with all the necessary items for a pleasant visit, insisting that Libby keep everything, nightgown and all.

One particular trip, however, she ran into a problem. Traveling by herself between Ohio and Pennsylvania in the wee hours of the morning, she got sleepy. She noticed a large truck stop with a bright neon light that spelled out **Hot Coffee**. She pulled her van into the truck stop, purchased a coffee and a Danish, and went back into the van to sleep. An hour later, she was abruptly awakened by a pounding on her van window and a police officer shouting, "Ma'am, please step out of the van."

"Wha?...huh? What's the problem, Officer?" Libby stumbled over her words while arousing herself from her deep sleep.

"What are you doing in this parking lot by yourself so late at night, Ma'am?" he questioned.

"Well, Officer, I'm just having a cup of coffee

and a little shut eye," she said.

"You will be arrested for vagrancy and soliciting if you stay here. You cannot sleep in this car." The officer had mistakenly thought that here slept a woman, either a vagrant, or worse, a prostitute, trying to solicit business outside the truck stop. Libby stepped out of the van and grabbing her wallet full of cash said, "No, Officer, I have money. See, here's my money. I just got tired and pulled off the road to sleep a bit. I'm not doing anything wrong."

After taking a good look at her, the police officer realized that she was telling the truth, and that she was not a bum or a prostitute. He asked her, "Lady, aren't you afraid to sleep here? This is a dangerous spot, especially for a woman."

She sweetly replied, "My good man (a common expression that she used when addressing strangers), I'm not afraid of anything."

That, in fact, was the truth. She wasn't afraid of too much. Even with the warning from the officer, in years to come, if she found herself getting tired on one of her solo road trips, she would pull into a truck stop and sleep. She firmly maintained that truck stops had the best coffee and breakfast at a good price. No matter how much money Libby made in later years, she didn't like to spend much money on food. She also didn't like to follow any provincial way of thinking. Her conflict was ongoing: the desire to be a free-spirit with no responsibility, and the need to fit into the traditional life that she observed in her mother, sisters, and women friends. To be sure, both of her sisters had a little of the gypsy spirit in them, especially Annette, but they managed to live the role of the typical housewife of the 1950s and 1960s. Their husbands knew that after a long day at work, in this case the Goodyear Rubber Factory, they would come home to a clean house, a spectacular meal, and more importantly, their wives would be there watching the children.

Libby was different. Having been widowed and remarried, this mother of two tried to play that role. She really did. It simply wasn't easy for her. She hated what she saw as a prosaic life. Had she been born at another time, or in a more progressive community, perhaps her needs and wants as a woman would not have been in such conflict. But she was a wife and mother of the 1950s, and in those days, America demanded a traditional role for its women. This tension manifested itself in many ways, especially with household chores. As Libby grew older, she settled down, to a certain extent, to a more traditional role, or maybe it can be said that at least in later years of her life, she enjoyed having a lovely home and maintaining that home. But in her early years as a housewife she had sporadic cleaning habits that could only be referred to as "cleaning frenzies." The daily routine of housekeeping was just too mundane for her. She would have preferred putting up dry wall, or some work project rather than play the role of homemaker. So she would let things get out of hand: dishes, dusting, cleaning bathrooms, etc. Then when things got too messy, with the help of several lady friends, they would clean the house top to bottom until the floors shined, the furniture smelled of freshly applied wax, and the bathrooms and kitchens sparkled. Since Libby had built the house with two complete living quarters to augment her income as a widow, the house was quite an ordeal to maintain, especially for a woman who hated household chores. The house consisted of two full kitchens, two bathrooms, two living rooms, four bedrooms, one large dining room, and a gigantic basement and attic. The cleaning frenzy was quite needed. When this frenzy ended, the immaculate condition of the house would last for a while until the house and its cleanliness, once again, got out of hand and then the same cleaning spurt would commence.

This procedure applied to washing and ironing clothes, too. She simply couldn't see doing these terribly boring tasks on a weekly basis. Instead, her routine was to wear the clothes, get them dirty, and then put them in a large pile in the basement. When the pile got too high, and the need for clean clothes surfaced, she would pack these soiled clothing items in large boxes and take them to a woman, who for a slight fee, would wash and press the clothes using a machine called a mangle. The results were lovely: perfectly washed and pressed clothes packed neatly in boxes. Mom was happy, for even though she didn't like to maintain the clothes, she absolutely loved looking good, and in some small way, she felt that she had truly helped this woman, the "washing lady," by giving her the much needed money.

This way of life changed with a twist of irony. God, many times, seems to have a sense of humor, and he certainly showed a sense of humor in the immediate relatives that surrounded Libby. Not only was she the daughter of a traditional housewife mother with impeccable cleaning habits, but my sister and I were "neat freaks." As we grew older, and even as she grew older and more settled, the house was always clean, clothes were washed, and for all practical purposes, it was a traditionally kept house that would have made even her mother proud. Libby, however, couldn't quite break herself from the habit of the "cleaning frenzy," so periodically, a dear family friend named Milka, who was more like a whirling dervish, cleaned the house with a vengeance. In spite of her gruff manner she endeared herself to all of us. In the midst of her cleaning, she would yell at us, "What's this doing here? What kind of mess is this? Come on, all of you, now let's clean this up!"

Worthy of the immaculately cleaned kitchens of the Slavic people, you could have eaten on Milka's floors. When I married and moved out of the home years later, my mother continued to rely on this cleaning wonder, Milka, to keep the house in order. Milka didn't drive a car. So the cleaning favor was reciprocated: Mom would pick Milka up and drive her to many places and events. Once again, mutual needs were met, and everybody was happy.

More than anything else, the gypsy spirit was best demonstrated in my mother's desire to play music and to be on the road.

Chapter 22...Playing in the Band

Oj ti pile, slave pile   (O my little chick, sweet chick)
Ja sam pevi jedna pesma (I will sing you a song)

Close to two years after our New York vacation, Mom approached me and informed me that, once again, it was time to get serious about forming a band. "Stace, it's time that you quit the youth orchestra and put all those music lessons to some good use." With the New York fiasco relatively fresh in my memory, I prodded for more information, "I'm not following you, Mom. What do you mean?"

It's time that we seriously started a band. Dedo Moisoff played music in a band, your Uncle Bobby played music in a band, and now you and I are going to play music in a band and because you play the *prim*, you will be the lead instrumentalist."

I pleaded that I was only fourteen years old, but age didn't matter in Mom's grand plans. Immediately, she visited the local musician's union office to secure memberships for us, paid the yearly fee, and listed our names as both tamburitzan players and guitarists. Opportunities to play slowly trickled in, so to increase the musical jobs, Mom devised a lucrative marketing plan. Recognizing that she needed a unique idea and sound to make a mark in the music field, she began recruiting for what would be her all girls' band which she called Libby's All Girl Tamburitzan Orchestra. In 1965, in Youngstown, Ohio, this was a novel idea. Her first recruit was the bass player, whom we all called Kuma Helen. In Macedonian, Serbian, and Croatian cultures, when anyone stood as the sponsor as a baby was baptized, that person, if she was a female was called *Kuma* or godmother; if a male, *Kum* or godfather. The relationship was very close, just as close as any blood line. Any other members of that person's family were referred to as *kumovi*. Neither Helen nor my mother were true *kumovi*. Helen had been one of the witnesses and the matron of honor at my mother's second marriage. But godmother or not, we always addressed her as Kuma Helen. Her contributions to the band were many: she spoke the language, sang, and played a mean upright bass.

The next recruit for the orchestra was a highly unlikely choice: a school teacher from my elementary school, Patty Zbell, who later joined the faculty at the reputable Grove City College. Accustomed to living a quiet, academic life, Patty experienced a great deal of adventure as the friend of Libby Moisoff George Fill. Mom placed a cello in Patty's hands and gave her basic lessons. The cello in a tamburitzan orchestra is not like the typical cello in a symphony orchestra. This cello, with its low sounding tones, is played with a pick, and the notes are plucked out in "musical runs" that enhance the rhythm of the bass as well as mellow out the high sounding tones of the prim. Some tamburitzan orchestras do not use a cello, but when they do, the instrument provides a finishing, or more polished sound to the tamburitzan orchestra consisting of an upright bass played with a pick, a *bugaria* (for chords), a *prim* and a *brac* (pronounced *brach)* for the melody and harmony instrumentations.

The next two choices for the band members were easy for her: First, her niece Sandy, daughter of her elder sister, Annette. Sandy boasted beauty queen status, having won many pageants and titles in the Akron, Ohio area. Even though Sandy wasn't a tamburitzan instrumentalist, she had an exceptional voice, played the guitar, and possessed a dynamic stage personality. Finally, making good on her edict that I would play in the band, as a skinny, ninth grader with braces on my teeth, I started playing music professionally. It wasn't something that I wanted to do. Oh, I loved music, but I wanted to play music as a hobby, not a job. At that age, I preferred to play music with the youth orchestras, but apparently, that was not the plan for my life. Even though the musical engagements offered opportunities that few teenage girls experienced, the life style of a young musician often conflicted with my desire to be the all-American girl participating in normal activities such as cheerleading, student council, French club, etc.

On one occasion, the orchestra had a job that started at 9:00 P.M., but I was cheerleading at a basketball game that went into overtime. As a young high school girl, cheerleading was the world to me, but to my mother, even though she was a sports enthusiast, musical engagements, or gigs, had preeminence certainly over a high school basketball game. I saw it otherwise. That evening Mom packed my instrument in the car and wearing her typical musician's outfit of black pants, white shirt, and colorful vest, she boldly strutted into the high school gymnasium, right next to the railing in the stands. Proudly wearing my pleated red and black short, cheerleading skirt and red sweater with CMHS sewn in bold black letters standing for my beloved Campbell Memorial High School, I was in the middle of a cheerleading routine in the center of the basketball court. Waving her arms emphatically, she motioned for me to leave the basketball court. I turned my head the other way, ignoring her. I wanted to cheer. She started to call my name very loudly! Recognizing that this had the potential to be a very embarrassing situation, I walked over to the railing where she was leaning. With a frozen smile on her face she said, "Get off this basketball court now and come and play music before I come down and get you!" An idle threat, this was not, so I scurried off the basketball court to the bewilderment of my cheerleading squad. I pouted that entire evening, but nevertheless, I obeyed my mother and played the job, not quitting until 2:00 A.M. When it came to playing music, Mom always called the shots, telling us what to wear, what to play, when to take a break, and when to quit. Since we were all young teenagers, we followed her commands. We called her the *gazdaritsa*—Slavic for big boss lady. The orchestra was her kingdom, and she was the reigning monarch. For that matter, Mom just naturally took to being the *gazdaritsa* in most situations. The role suited her well. Even at restaurants, Mom took it upon herself to order for everyone. When the waitress would come to our table to take the order, Mom would stop her from asking each individual what they wanted. She would say to all of us, "Don't confuse the waitress, just order pork chops and applesauce for everyone." It got to be a family joke, and we would tease one another with, "Pork chops and applesauce for everyone," imitating the voice of WC Fields as we said it. Mom possessed charisma and naturally drew people to her, but make no mistake—she was the one in charge of any situation. It was probably this strong characteristic that helped her to overcome any obstacles in her life.

Things weren't always that dramatic. Over the years, the band took on different musicians. Girls were just a difficult group to keep together. Boyfriends, husbands, and babies often caused the group dynamics to change, but the constants in those early years were always Mom and I.

As the years progressed, the quality of the musicianship of the band members got better and better, the jobs became more impressive, and I started to have fun. It was an honor to play music with both Patty Zbell and Kuma Helen, but I thrived on the duets with my cousin Sandy, and I was ecstatic over the incredible new musicians that joined the band. Four girls who were all my age and could play just about any instrument joined our orchestra: Eileen and Kathy Zadravec (who were sisters), Peggy Namesnik, and Darlene Balog. Sometimes we used a violinist from Canton, Ohio named Marie Bilon. The music had an intoxicating gypsy sound to it, yet we could revert to playing classical, traditional, and Gospel musical selections upon request.

Besides our following, which became quite large, we had our own intimate entourage, those faithful family members and friends that followed us everywhere and made the job more pleasant for all of us. In the early days of the band, our special friends John and Dorothy Kushner and their son Ron, Sandy's parents and her sister Annette, who was named after her mother, came to most of our musical bookings. It was Annette, fondly called Nettie, who often stepped in as the stabilizing force in my life as I played, especially when the jobs became difficult or too demanding. I always struggled with wanting to play music and wanting to simply lead the normal life of a teenage girl. Nettie seemed to sense when I needed a word of encouragement, or just a good laugh. Two years older than I, we would remain the best of friends, as well as cousins, for life.

Once when I was in junior high, a young teenage boy had won a stuffed animal for me at the local church bazaar. I was so excited. To think that a boy had won something for me! I came home with my prize and ran to put it in my room, but before I reached my room my mom stopped me and said, "You're too old for that stuffed animal; give it to your little sister Sally—she wants it." I would do anything for Sally, but this was my prize. I was crushed, and I began to sob. Nettie, who was visiting, took me aside and said, "Stace, give it to Sally. You're going to have lots and lots of boys who win things for you. I promise you." I believed her and willingly gave Sally my prize. With one sentence, Nettie had given me an affirmation of my value and a hope for good things to come. I just adored her. She had taken music lessons as a child, but she, like my stepdad, always remained in the background, allowing my mother, Sandy, and me to have center stage. We could always see her beaming at us as we performed.

Sandy and Annette's father, my Uncle Walter, was also a big fan of ours. He especially loved an instrumental piece called the *Romanian Rhapsody*, traditionally played by a violinist. He and my Tete Annette had a recording of this musical piece, but no musical score. Since I played the lead part in the orchestra on my mandolin-sounding instrument, the prim, Uncle Walter thought that I should learn to play this particular piece. Day after day, I listened to the record until I became quite comfortable with the song. I learned it completely by ear since we did not have a musical score for this piece. Whenever Uncle Walter attended one of our performances, he would give me a special smile, and I knew that it was time to play the *Romanian Rhapsody*. Because of the musical complexity of the instrumentation and probably because of my youth, I always received thunderous applause when the song ended. It gave Uncle Walter great pleasure to hear the applause, but it gave me great satisfaction to play it so well for him. Our performances grew in number as well as quality. The musical sound of our orchestra was very unique and we started getting bookings all over the United States. It was quite an interesting life style trying to blend my high school education and my teenage activities with playing music into the wee hours of the morning on weekends, as well as performing at evening concerts during the school week.

One particularly grueling "gig" occurred at a week long convention at the William Penn Hotel in Pittsburgh. With our instruments packed tightly in the car and the upright bass positioned between the front and back seats, Mom picked me up after the school day ended, and we made the two hour trek to Pittsburgh. We performed until midnight and then returned to our homes. I crawled into bed close to 3:00 A.M., only to wake up for school at 7:00 A.M. Mom never allowed me to miss school. Sitting in my first period French III class that morning, I was jolted from my stupor by the loud admonishing of the French teacher demanding me to pay attention and to get back to translating Guy de Maupassant's, *The Little Prince.*

It was expected of us, the young band members, to perform well on stage and to do well in school. Excuses and whining were not tolerated. It was a great training ground for the busyness of life, and it trained us to work with different personality types. Mom, by far, was the celebrity or diva of our orchestra. With her charismatic personality, she automatically drew people to her like a magnet. For her, it wasn't just playing music; it was the whole idea of being on stage and making people happy. Possessing this uncanny ability to remember special events and situations in people's lives, she would mention people in the audience by name with a special anecdote or statement that just pleased them immensely. One time we were playing at a fund raiser when a prominent funeral director from the area came into the room. She halted the music and jokingly shouted into the microphone, "Oh, Oh! There's Mr. Vaschak the funeral director! Hey, Mr. Vaschak, you better stay away from me. I'm turning sideways so that you don't size me up." The audience, including Mr. Vaschak, howled. Although Mom enjoyed the celebrity, the jobs weren't about money. She did hundreds of jobs for charities: nursing homes, hospitals, handicapped children's homes, hospices, fund raisers, etc.

Once her connection with her audience backfired. We were playing for a senior citizen's center in Youngstown. Mom brought a cordless microphone to this particular job. As we walked around the room with our instruments, she would ask the residents of the center to tell her their nationality or ancestry. Then she would have us surround the person, letting that person sing into the microphone as we played his or her special ethnic song. While magical for the individual, it really caused us to draw on all our improvisational skills as we played on demand Italian

Tarantella's, German waltzes, Hungarian *Czardas,* Old Southern Gospel tunes, and every folk song imaginable from such countries as Poland, Africa, Slovakia, Croatia, Serbia, Ireland, and completing the repertoire with the difficult syncopated rhythms of the Mideast: Greek, Macedonian, Bulgarian, Lebanese, and Israeli. It was a musical version of the United Nations, and one that truly promoted peace and unity. This went on for over an hour.

Finally, we came to a man who requested an Irish ballad. When we started playing "When Irish Eyes Are Smiling," the man, who had a decent tenor voice, joined us. Mom had the man beaming with pride when she shouted to the audience, "Wow! This man is really good! What an Irish tenor! The next time I come, Sir, I'm going to take you on the road with me." Of course, she was only joking.

A month later, we came back for our charitable service at the senior center. The staff, who adored my mother, looked nervous. "What's the matter?" asked Mom. They pointed to the man, our Irish tenor, who was waiting for her with his suitcase packed and ready to go on tour! It was a delicate situation to amend, but Mom with her charm, graciously wiggled out of it, although henceforth, she would carefully curb her wit at the nursing home.

~

Our band continued to prosper and the natural course of action was to make a record. Record sales, in the realm of tamburitzan music, were excellent, but unlike other ethnic musical groups, for instance, *River Dance*, our ethnic music didn't seem to cross over into the mainstream of the music world on a grand scale. However, some of our accomplishments were pretty significant. We made records, performed nationally, were on the radio; in fact, my mother was hired as a radio announcer and had her own radio program on two different stations in Youngstown, Ohio, which earned her much celebrity in a tri-state area, as well as national celebrity in the Slavic world. She was inducted into the national Tamburitzan Hall of Fame. Her radio and music career spanned close to sixty years. But the summer of 1976 opened the door for the most exciting musical endeavor of our orchestra.

That summer we received an invitation to perform at the American Folklife Bicentennial Celebration in Washington, D.C. The promoter of this event was quite visionary. For every international music ensemble that he hired, he booked a corresponding American folk orchestra. For instance, he matched an Italian-American ensemble with an Italian ensemble from Italy, or he paired an Irish-American quartet with a Celtic band from Ireland. Quite innovating, this method was applied to dozens of ethnic bands and groups. They matched us with an ensemble from Skopje, Macedonia, with whom we befriended. It was quite an honor for us. Because of Mom's fluency in Macedonian, she communicated with them quite well. I fumbled with the syntax of the language, sounding something like my Grandmother Annastasia did when she attempted to speak English, only this time it was reversed: I was trying to convert English into Macedonian. Despite my difficulty, I got my ideas across in my rudimentary Macedonian. The Macedonian girls, who were dancers, marveled at our ability as women to play tamburitzan instruments. In their ensemble, only the men played the instruments while the women danced. We joked and said, "This is America. Women can do anything here." Certainly, in our case, that was true.

This summer engagement led to an incredible musical opportunity. Hearing our band, a member of the Inaugural Committee for Cultural Events hired us to perform at the National Visitor's Center in Washington during the Inaugural celebrations. The invitation bore the signature of President-elect Jimmy Carter. We readily accepted and began preparing for this esteemed event. We arrived in our nation's capital on what had to be one of the coldest January days that the Washington, DC area had experienced in quite some time. But all that was forgotten when President Jimmy Carter entered the ballroom to the sounds of *Hail to the Chief.*

Here we stood in the same room as the President of the United States, and we performed songs and played instruments that reflected our heritage, birthed in that remote village in Macedonia. Tears streamed down our cheeks as we, descendants of Macedonian immigrants, used our talents to celebrate the inauguration of an American President. The evening seemed like a dream and was over far too soon.

Chapter 23...
Finding A New Route

Izgubljano (Lost lamb)

Playing music in the band had many benefits, but there were a few negative aspects. For one thing, we always got lost. My mother had absolutely no sense of direction, never followed a map, and refused to believe that she didn't know where she was going. It usually started when entering a toll road of any given state. When the road forked into two directions marked east or west, Mom repeatedly, almost instinctively, would go the wrong way. Once we had completed a job in Cleveland, Ohio, and we needed to head east to Youngstown. It was November, and we found ourselves in a major Cleveland snowstorm, its fierceness brought on by the close proximity to Lake Erie. Visibility was minimal, but that didn't stop Mom from driving full speed ahead. She simply had no fear! Traveling with us was an older musician, who had joined us for this special occasion in Cleveland. He kept droning on and on about the glory days of by-gone musicians. Mom kept driving through the blizzard, laughing and fondly reminiscing with him. The windshield wipers were totally ineffective by this time. As we approached the green road sign that posted those vitally needed directions, I gasped as I saw "Columbus—two miles." We had traveled close to two hours going the wrong direction! This wasn't the first time; it wouldn't be the last. This pattern would be repeated in West Virginia, Wisconsin, Virginia, New York, Michigan, Indiana—just to name a few states. Jokingly, I accused her of trying to provide equal opportunity for us to be lost in each state. Wouldn't want to leave any state out! Although, truthfully, I inherited those same genes for getting lost, and she impishly would remind me of that fact.

One particularly serious time of "lostness" occurred in the wild and wonderful state of West Virginia. As Midwesterners accustomed to flat land where you can look straight ahead and see your destination, West Virginia, with its winding roads and mountainous altitudes, challenged our equilibrium and sense of direction. Driving through this terrain, Mom, as the lead driver in a caravan of cars, insisted that her gut feeling was right which, of course, we all knew was far from the truth. But, she was the *gazdaritisa*—the big boss lady. To minimize the tension, we evoked our long-standing restaurant joke, "Don't confuse the waitress—pork chops and applesauce for everyone." The idea was to do whatever she said and just laugh about it. After a while, however, nothing was very funny to us. We spent hours traveling on remote roads without a clue of where we were or where we were going. It wasn't a matter of stopping to ask for directions: there was no one to ask in this apparently uninhabited area of West Virginia. The alliterated state promotional motto of "wild and wonderful West Virginia" took on a new meaning for us. Any road trip after a musical performance was grueling, let alone one accompanied by hours of being lost. By the time we reached the hotel, we were short-tempered, motion sick, and simply exhausted.

As we settled into sleeping arrangements at a shabby motel in the backwoods of West Virginia, we had a party of twelve, including the band. Somehow we managed to split that group of twelve into two rooms. My mother, who really was a generous and big spender in most situations, always cut corners when it came to restaurants and hotel accommodations. So, our group of twelve, in true *Ciganke* (gypsy) style, sprawled themselves over beds, cots, and floors in the two rooms. Since we had to leave early the next morning for our job, we asked one of the members of our party who was in another room to give us a wake-up call. Early the next morning she made a phone call to our room. The phone rang and rang. I heard it. Didn't everyone hear it?

No one answered. Stumbling over sleeping bodies in my state of semi-alertness, I picked up the receiver. A voice that sounded vaguely familiar inquired, "Good morning, who is this?" I started to say my name, but I was so exhausted that I absolutely could not remember who I was. I desperately looked at everyone else in the room and pleaded, "Who am I? Who am I?" Everyone now totally awake started to laugh and yell, "You're Stacie!" I snapped out of my sleeping stupor and spoke confidently into the phone, "This is Stacie."

~

Not only did my family have trouble with directions, cars and their proper maintenance ran a close second. Wrecking a car could never be classified as a genetic behavior, and few psychologists would spend time writing a thesis on "Wrecking Cars: A Learned Behavior." Yet, in our family, I sometimes wonder. It started with my Grandfather Dimko. In 1912 when Dimko came to Campbell, Ohio and settled in a tiny company home at the top of a hill, he didn't worry about, or even consider transportation. He simply walked to the bottom of the hill where the "Campbell Works" of the massive Youngstown Sheet and Tube Company was located. Walking back up the hill, one of the few large hills in the state of Ohio, he stopped at a local store where one of his buddies, Tomo, persuaded him to buy his car. Tomo gave his sale's pitch: "Come, on. This be *beeauteeful* car. Go *anyvere*. Up hill. Down hill. *Vat* you *vaiting* for? You no have car--I have car... *To bija dobro* (It's all good). *Vat* you say, Dimko?"

The man desperately needed money, and Dimko never could refuse anybody anything. He bought this car and proudly drove it home—up the big hill. The car worked adequately, for a while, and then it abruptly stopped running. Not possessing any mechanical skills, his plan was simple and precise: He tried starting the car. When it wouldn't start, he kicked both sides of the car, raging as he hurt his foot. His decision was inevitable, and to him, completely logical: Uttering a few choice Macedonian expletives, he rolled the car down over the hill! He never turned around to look as it crashed, fortunately, not causing any major damage to anyone. It would be years before he purchased another vehicle.

~

A generation later, the wrecking of cars lived on with his daughter Libby. She purchased a brand new *Open Road* van. Since she had driven so many "bombs" in her life, she was quite proud of this spanking new, blue and white van. With a small bathroom, a sink, and accommodations for sleeping four, it was truly her home away from home. More than that, it sufficiently accommodated her musical orchestra of four, as well as instruments, microphones, and speakers. This new van alleviated the spatial dilemma of positioning the big, upright bass between the front and back seats of her smaller car.

But this time, it wasn't being used for a musical engagement. No, this time she was on an outing with me. Mother and daughter were having an amiable ride until we reached Pittsburgh, Pennsylvania and had to park the large van in a parking garage. The problem was that the *Open Road* had an extended top that increased the vehicle's height close to the clearance limits of most parking garages. As we approached the entrance of the garage, I noticed a sign posted: **Low Clearance.** I nervously asked, "Mom, don't you think the Open Road is too high for this garage?"

Mom responded, "Nope, we got lots of room."

I repeated, "Mom, no really—I think it's too high. I don't think that we can clear it."

Mom, "Oh, sure, we can. It's not too high. You always worry about something. Why can't you be more like me—I never worry." That was true. She didn't have to worry; I worried enough for both of us. But my pleading continued, "Mom, I really think the van is too high, and I don't think you should go in there."

"Be quiet and let me drive; I don't need a back seat driver! It'll fit!" I tightly closed my eyes as my mother, driving full speed ahead, rammed into the ceiling of the parking garage nearly ripping the top off her beloved blue *Open Road* van!

The parking attendant raced over and frantically yelled, "Lady, are you crazy? Didn't you see the sign? Couldn't you tell that your van was too high?"

Amazed though I was over our escape from injury, I smugly added, "See, I told you that the van was too high." Satisfaction on my part, silence on hers. However, the pinnacle of car catastrophes, also involving the beloved *Open Road,* occurred in my driveway in Pennsylvania. By this time, I was married with a home and family of my own. While visiting me, Mom parked her van in the driveway, located on a hill overlooking a local community college. For some odd reason, she didn't believe in using her emergency brake. Ever. It actually annoyed her if anyone who drove her van put the emergency brake on. This time was no exception, but she neglected to factor in one element in her way of thinking: emergency brakes may not be tremendously needed in the flat state of Ohio, but on Pennsylvanian hills, they are handy tools. It was around midnight when our sleeping household was awakened by a strange tremor accompanied by a loud thud. The sound came from the north side of our house and my husband, in a semi-awakened state, glanced out the window just in time to witness a most peculiar sight. In what seemed like slow motion, the *Open Road* started to go forward, minus a driver, and after scraping the brown brick on the side of the house, traveled down the driveway, down the hill through the trees, crossed the street, and abruptly halted when it hit a telephone pole located on the college property that was some distance from our back yard. Waking up to this surrealistic scene, all inhabitants of the household, including Mom, rushed outside running after the van. The neighbors, awakened by the loud sound of the van hitting the telephone pole, ran out of their own homes. As the startled group met at the bottom of the hill, there was a moment of complete silence. Then a boisterous laugh was heard. Bewildered, everyone turned around to try to discover the source of this laughter. It was Mom laughing hysterically and shouting, "Hee Hee Hee—Herbie Rides Again! The van wanted to go to college!" By this time, the cluster of neighbors, dressed in their nightclothes added their voices to her laughter. Fortunately, no one was hurt. Damage was minimal, and Mom continued to drive that van for years to come! Until the van was properly buried at a junk yard years later, the family always referred to it as Herbie, after the *Volkswagon* from the Disney movie. In that movie, Herbie rode without the need of a driver, likewise the *Open Road.*

~

Not only did she wreck cars, Mom accumulated a good number of tickets while driving, or in some cases, parking. Believing that she had the right to park her car just about anywhere she wanted, the result was an accumulation of parking tickets, which eventually landed her in court. The judge in a somber tone questioned her, "Ma'am, I just don't understand all these tickets. Do you have any explanation for this?"

"Well, Judge, you see, Judge, I just can't seem to find places to park, and well, I have my elderly Aunt Frances here, as she pointed to one of her elderly relatives who had accompanied her to this trial. "She can't walk very far." Mom was shrewd. She understood imaging, and this image of Tete Francis hunched over from osteoporosis induced sympathy.

The judge responded quickly, "I understand that, Ma'am, but there are rules, and these rules must be followed. You should have applied for a handicapped parking permit if that were the issue. I just don't know what to think here, Mrs. Fill. You seem like a reasonably nice lady, and I can understand your problem." He paused and reflected for a few seconds and then asked:

"Mrs. Fill, what do you think **I** should do with **you**?" Mom couldn't believe the question, so she repeated it, "What do **I** think you should do with me?"

"Yes, Mrs. Fill, that is what I said," reiterated the judge.

"Well," Mom responded, "**I** think that you should let me go." And she thought to herself, "Silly man. What does he think I should say?" Strangely enough, the bemused judge let her go with just a warning. Tickets, wrecked cars, and hours traveling on roads lost seemed to be the routine for Mom, especially when she played music. But despite these obstacles, a life as a musician did have its perks.

Chapter 24...Going to College

L'esprit du Duc
Duquesne University, Pittsburgh, Pennsylvania

Even though our girls' band was quite successful, the greatest achievement connected with
playing tamburitzan music for me was admission as
a college student into the internationally acclaimed
Duquesne University Tamburitzans. Not only was
Duquesne University a highly respected private
university, the tamburitzans as a musical ensemble
were known worldwide. Every young tamburitzan
player in America, and even overseas, recognized
the Duquesne University Tamburitzans, whose home
base is in Pittsburgh, Pennsylvania, as the preemi-
nent tamburitzan ensemble. To be accepted into its
ranks for tamburitzan players is equivalent to accep-
tance into the top ballet company in the world. In
fact, the dancers of the Duquesne University
Tamburitzans often trained with choreographers
from the top ballet companies and folk dancing

ensembles internationally, including the state ensembles of Russia, Romania, Hungary, and Bulgaria whose discipline in the art of dance and dancing techniques was legendary.

From childhood, each year I would attend a performance by the Duquesne ensemble. When I was in tenth grade, I attended one of their performances which was followed by a dance reception. I was captivated by the musicianship of several members of their "combo" that played for dancing entertainment, particularly a musician and lead vocalist named Steve Vesolich.

Yep, I had decided that this was the direction for me, so I made plans to audition for the "Tammies" as they were fondly called. But that was tenth grade. In my junior and senior years of high school, I became serious about appearing as the "all-American girl." My high school experience provided me with many opportunities to do so: cheerleader, homecoming queen, class queen, yearbook editor, newspaper columnist—all those great moments and achievements of the high school life that seemed so important at that time—and meant so little later in life. Unlike many people who moan about the terrible years endured in high school, it was a thrilling time for me, and I loved every minute of it.

I also loved to watch Ohio State football, especially with their yearly visits to the Rose Bowl under the coaching of Woody Hayes. As part of the Big Ten, the Ohio State Buckeyes made the game seem bigger than life. This love for football, particularly college ball, started with my cheerleading days when friends of my parents noticed that I was yelling "DEFENSE!" when our team's offensive line was moving. The friend teased, "Hey, Libby and Cas, doesn't your daughter know anything about football? Listen to her cheering. She doesn't know the offense from the defense." My embarrassed parents, knowledgeable football enthusiasts themselves, sat me down that next Saturday during an Ohio State football game and gave me a play by play description of the mechanics of the game. I loved to watch football games from that moment on.

As I approached my senior year of high school, rather than auditioning for Duquesne University and the Tamburitzans as I had planned to do in tenth grade, I decided that I wanted to be a cheerleader at the colossal OSU. I had spent a weekend as a "little sister" with my cousins Annette and Sandy who went to Ohio State. The year was 1969; the youth of America were in rebellion, and I was swept away with the energy of that gigantic American university, more like its own major city. As America's youth rebelled, I felt that this was not the time to draw on my ethnic roots. I was the "all-American girl" now, and I wanted to live out that persona, even though I was highly involved with the music and life of the Slavic community, which truly existed as its own culture within the American culture. We Slavic teens joked that we were American kids from Monday to Friday from 7:00 A.M. to 3:00 P.M., but after school and on weekends, we moved in a completely different culture than the typical American teenager. All that temporarily changed for me when I visited Ohio State University.

After returning from that fun-packed weekend with my cousins, my conversation with my mother was a blunt one, "Mom, I've decided to go to Ohio State. I think that I'll be a cheerleader there." The comment to my mother was quite audacious, bordering on the absurd. First of all, to my knowledge, most of the cheerleaders at Ohio State were trained gymnasts, physical education majors, or at least incredibly talented athletes. I was not. I was a musician, a singer— a dancer.

Secondly, just the week before my visit to Ohio State, I had confidently informed my mother that I wanted to audition for a position as part of the water skiing team at Sea World in Aurora, Ohio. Waterskiing comprised one of the three athletic events besides dancing in which I was proficient: swimming, ice skating, and water skiing. My family teased me about my ability to stay remarkably balanced on one ski as the boat raced at top speed: "You only stay up because you are afraid of fish and don't want to fall into the lake," they joked. That was probably true. But in my youthful, and a tad arrogant thinking, I now envisioned a career as a water skier at Sea World.   In a very short span of time, I capriciously had contemplated career choices ranging from a tamburitzan at Duquesne University, a water skier at Sea World, and a cheerleader at Ohio State University. Mom must have chuckled to herself, but she played it cool. She simply said, "Well, that's OK, but you know the Duquesne University Tamburitzans are having auditions soon, and they offer complete college scholarships including tuition, room and board, books, and the opportunity to travel. They are taking in three new freshman girls. It would be a good experience for you. Give it a try; if it doesn't work, you haven't lost anything." Since the auditions that year involved close to two hundred people, it would, indeed, be a good experience. I could make a decision later, I thought.

I began to prepare for my audition. I would need to showcase three talents for this audition: singing, dancing, and instrumentation. I diligently prepared my selections. Since the Duquesne University Tamburitzans are primarily known for their featured Serbo-Croat, Macedonian, and Bulgarian dancing (areas of familiarity to me), I decided to focus on something that I thought was not as familiar to the ensemble: I drew on my Greek heritage and choreographed a version of *Zorba the Greek*. Then I painstakingly worked on an orchestration number that featured my skills at playing the prim. Finally, I prepared a vocal selection, a lovely soprano folk song entitled *Ima Teli Pari* that bemoaned the tale of a gypsy girl who had no money.

The day of the audition arrived. We traveled the two hours to Pittsburgh, my loyal band members making the trip with me to provide background orchestration. Upon arriving, most of the students who planned to audition took a few moments to "regroup" before auditioning. Not me. I exited from the car and went right to the judges sitting in the front row. I never bothered to comb my hair or re-apply makeup to give myself a fresher look. I was here to showcase my musical, vocal, and dance qualities, and I wanted to get down to business. My name was called and they told me to go on stage. In that panel of judges sat the director, the vocal instructor, the head choreographer, and several guys who were seniors, among them that young man that I had observed two years ago—Steve Vesolich.

I began the audition with my Greek dance. My back up band was wonderful, and I started to have fun with the choreography. When the dance was over, the choreographer asked if I knew traditional Balkan dances. When I said that I did, he asked one member of the ensemble to go on stage and dance with me. I was having a great time. The dancer was a young man named Jonathan Fister who lived only a short distance from my home town. I had known him for years. I was feeling confident in my audition. Next, I sang my vocal selection. Strong. Loud. My voice wasn't shaky.

Of all the elements of the audition, my instrumentation was the area that I felt the most confident. I could play my little prim in my sleep. This beloved instrument that I had played since I was a child was like an appendage to me. But adrenalin makes you do funny things. I began to play my selection, a very difficult piece of music, but one that I had done quite adeptly dozens of times. Suddenly, my right hand felt like lead. The instrumentation required skillful fingering as well as a tricky movement of my right hand and the pick. I felt that I could barely move my hand. Usually the left hand which does the fingering is more difficult, but this time, and totally catching me off guard, it was my right hand. I labored through this portion of the audition. My back up band, which consisted of my mother and those faithful girls in the orchestra who had shared the stage with me hundreds of times, played powerfully to give me support. It wasn't my best instrumental performance. To make matters worse, in my nervousness I started moving my hip as I was playing, just a little twist. If I had looked up at the senior boys during my audition, I would have noticed the smiles on their faces and the raised eyebrows they were giving me. My little twist of the hip was turning into quite a little sexy movement. I was totally unaware of this. I was just trying to get through my instrumentation.

The audition was over. We left the stage, loaded our instruments, and went home. I didn't know what to think. But I had a few more months of high school, and there was always Ohio State. By this time, I had wisely discarded any thoughts about auditioning for Sea World, and my parents, to their credit, never giggled in my presence over this ridiculous idea.

In April, I got the results of my college boards, quite acceptable scores for Duquesne University. Then a most astonishing letter arrived: I had been accepted into the esteemed Duquesne University Tamburitzans, and I was granted a full scholarship to the university. The letter reiterated what my mother had told me: the scholarship included room and board, tuition, books, and the opportunity to travel all over the United States. I quickly forgot about Ohio State, thus ending my cheerleading ambitions.

After I got into the troupe, the guys who had attended the audition teased me about my little "hip movement" calling it the cutest thing that they had ever seen. They also recognized that I had talent, even though it truly wasn't highlighted during that audition. What I didn't know was that the director was quite familiar with my work as a member of the all girls' band, so he had confidence in my ability. I had caught his attention. I also caught the attention of an incredibly talented person: Steve Vesolich.

Chapter 25...Going to Camp

Here I am at Camp Nebagamon!

Members of the Duquesne University Ensemble left every August for a rigorous artistic training camp in Lake Nebagamon, Wisconsin. The idea was to remove the performers from any city distractions and to place them in a quaint, Wisconsin camp setting where they focused on dancing, singing, and instrumentation. Musical directors, vocal coaches, and choreographers from all over the world arrived at camp with the performers. Preparation for the show demanded hours and hours of practice time. The final product, a two hour production, had to flow perfectly before the troupe would leave camp since this production would be performed over one hundred times during the college school year and nightly during special spring, summer, and fall tours. When the Tamburitzans, fondly called the Tammies, performed in the States, the flavor of the show boasted a Southern Slavic repertoire. Instrumentation included tamburas, violins, flutes, Russian balalaikas, accordions, and exotic Eastern European instruments such as the *gajde*, a bagpipe made from goat skins. Ethnic costumes were meticulously researched and replicated for authenticity. Choreographers with thick accents traveled thousands of miles from remote corners of the world to validate the accuracy of the folk dancing choreographies. When the Tammies performed abroad, however, the performance reflected an Americana theme. The overseas performance was a montage in chronological order of dance and music in America, from Early American contra dancing right through the decades, culminating in the current contemporary dance culture of the time. Soft, leather folk dancing shoes, called *Opanke,* were replaced with shoes for tap and swing. Colorful ethnic garb was neatly packed away in trunks as the seamstresses created dazzling costumes that authentically represented the various decades and geographical sections of America. More choreographers and vocal instructors were recruited to piece together this American quilt of dancing and music. This was the backdrop of my new world when I left for training camp as a young seventeen year old girl, two months out of high school.

My proud parents drove me to Pittsburgh to catch the Tammies' bus for Wisconsin, but we had a little extra time to have something to eat. Pittsburgh is a delightful town, and we found a quaint restaurant that offered steaks, salads, and baked potatoes for a reasonable price (Mom never liked to pay a lot of money at restaurants, of course). My suitcases, loaded with a wardrobe that I had spent weeks selecting, were squashed in the back compartment of our station wagon. The suitcases, locked securely in the hatchback, could easily be seen by anyone on the street, something that we small town suburbanites didn't deem important. We had played with temptation. When we returned to the car, we discovered that the car had been burglarized. The suitcases were gone! Not a trace.

Fortunately, I had kept my duffel bag with me when we had gone into the restaurant. It was filled with toiletries, cosmetics, and thankfully, clean underwear. But other than that, I left for a month of camp with only the clothes on my back. The majority of the female performers in the ensemble were petite and similarly built, so borrowing clothes, particularly clothes needed for dance rehearsal, was not a problem. For, the next month, as I trained at dance camp from early in the morning until late in the evening, wearing borrowed clothes, I would receive an interesting package at mail call every week. My mother, bless her heart, purchased new clothes and sent them to me since I didn't really have anything of my own to wear. Most teenage girls would be mortified at the thought of their moms selecting their entire wardrobes. For me, this proved to be true, especially with my mother's personal style which was part gypsy and definitely ALL glitzy! My mother was always the showman, and I guess she assumed that since I was in a performing ensemble, I would need "stage type" clothes. I, personally, leaned toward the typical style of dress of the early '70s: bell bottom jeans, "poorboy" tops, and mini-skirts that lacked a lot of fuss and muss. With great anticipation, the girls in my cottage at camp watched the unwrapping of each mail package that revealed a little dress with sequins, beads, and outlandish colors, I simply said thank you and borrowed clothes from my girlfriends until I was able to get back to Pittsburgh and make major purchases at Kaufmann's department store, so much so, that my bank account, actually my mother's account, was overdrawn. I guess we both were even.

The wardrobe situation was only one of the demanding elements of my indoctrination at the training camp of the Duquesne University Tamburitzan's ensemble. From the intensity of the training, my leg muscles ached, my throat throbbed, and I, who had tremendous energy and stamina, was exhausted. In addition, performers had to live the life of true campers, keeping their cottages sparkling clean. All chores were maintained, even when we crawled into bed in the wee hours of the morning after a performance.

During that first month of training, we presented our show to the locals as a means of "testing the water." Even though the audience recognized that these performances were glorified dress rehearsals, our director and his staff tolerated no errors. If a performer accidentally dropped a piece of his or her costume on stage during a performance, a fine was promptly charged. Every element of the performance was on a trial basis during that first month. If you earned a solo, but the director and his staff didn't feel that it flowed in the manner that they had designed, the number was cut. This occurred after weeks of practice when stress levels were high and the competitive nature of the camp was intense. The camp was not known for building self-esteem in individuals. In one of my earliest performances as a freshman, they took a publicity shot of me dancing a high-stepping Bulgarian choreography. In the photo, my hands were held high skillfully twirling a hanky, and there was a perfect smile on my face, unfortunately though, at the instant the photo was snapped, my foot dangled slightly lower than the other two dancers next to me, both senior girls. I was called into the director's office where the tell-tale photo was lying on his desk. He tapped at it with his finger, clearly showing me the horridness of my dancing sin. In a stern voice, he asked, "Do you see your foot?" I said nothing. He asked another question, "Do you see Cathy's foot? Now I want you to look closely to where Barb's foot is placed. Notice anything?" I still said nothing. I wanted to cry. But performers do not cry in front of artistic directors. They go back and they practice, and they don't make those same mistakes. That's what I did.

Camp came to an end. To regroup a bit, performers had some extra time to swim in the dark blue (and cold) water of Lake Nebagomen under clear skies. An old-fashioned corn roast and barbeque was scheduled with music and dancing—this time purely for recreation. In a sentimental gesture, the male performers of our troupe serenaded the women outside our cottage windows. I had survived training camp. It was August 27, 1969. I turned 18. An old boyfriend sent me a dozen red roses at camp. My parents surprised me by making the trip to camp to enjoy the lake, the camping, and to see me and the show (and, of course, to bring me more clothes). Many parents of the performers visited the camp. My parents were in for a surprise. My eyes and heart were turned in another direction, on that young man that I had seen on stage a few years before. His name was Steve Vesolich.

Chapter 26...
Finding A Love of My Own

A ti si srce mi   (And in my heart remains)
Tak puno sunce dala (a love that lives forever)
Ka morem ti nek rec (what more is there to say)
O sega srce fala   (with all my heart, I now thank you)

He was the lead vocalist and instrumentalist of the ensemble, a fifth year senior. As an under-classman, he had changed his major, but he could have completed his education in four years. He was such an extraordinary performer, however, that he was encouraged to take his time and stay an extra year with the ensemble, all this on full scholarship. Even after he graduated, he was asked to travel with the ensemble on tour, especially overseas. To me, this situation was a divine appointment. Had this talented performer graduated a year earlier, he would not have been in the group with me, but here I was, a freshman, and there he was, Steve Vesolich, the big man in the ensemble.

Steve, like any other suitor, wanted to win the approval of my parents who, at this time, vacationed in a cottage located about four blocks from the rehearsal auditorium in Lake Nebagamon. When he arrived for a visit with them at their rented cottage, Mom was frying the catch of the day: perch. She was pretty excited about it since my dad and sister Sally had caught the fish in the cold, clear waters of Lake Nebagamon. Steve's family were not big fish eaters, and he wasn't too eager to eat the fish, but ethnic women rarely take no for an answer when it comes to offering food. He politely accepted the plate of lightly breaded and fried perch from my mother. Whether she had been distracted, we don't know, but the fish wasn't completely cooked. Since he wasn't really knowledgeable about the taste of fresh fish, he politely ate the raw fish. It was terrible, but he never said one word. After he left, my mother nibbled on the leftover fish. She quickly spit it out when she realized it was raw! That was one of his first encounters with our family. Amazingly, it didn't scare him off.

I was eighteen; he was twenty two. That spring he graduated from Duquesne University with a BS in Education, specialty social studies. My parents were concerned that I wouldn't finish my education—that I would drop out of school to get married, but they underestimated my determination to receive my degree. Besides that, members of the Tammies were not permitted to get engaged and remain a member of the ensemble. I recognized the value of staying in school until graduation. The Tammies not only afforded me a quality education at no cost to me, but they provided opportunities to travel worldwide.

Although he had graduated, the staff often invited Steve to perform on overseas tours. Because of his new job teaching in a wonderful school district, Center Township, he occasionally would refuse these invitations. When he was not on tour with me, he carefully followed the tour's itinerary and timed it so that a letter or card from him would reach me in every city of the tour. On my nine-week tour to Greece, Bulgaria, France, and Czechoslovakia, the members of the troupe teased me during mail call:

"Here we go again, another love letter for Stacie from Steve," they lamented. He was not taking any chances. I was young, traveling with a troupe of forty performers of which over half were young men. He made sure that I didn't forget him while docked in some romantic setting on the French Riviera. The four years flew by and the second semester of my senior year approached. It had been a great year of accolades for me. In the fall of that year, I received the award for Outstanding Female Performer. In January, the Tammies performed at one of the Inaugural Balls of President Nixon (In my lifetime I had performed at two Presidential Inaugural Balls). My semester grades were quite respectable: a 4.0 GPA, and I had just completed a wonderful student teaching experience at a Pittsburgh school, West Mifflin High School. To end the school year on a high note, the Tammies performed at the majestic Heinz Hall in Pittsburgh. What a great finish to my college year when I was given a solo performance on the immense stage of Heinz Hall! This solo, a dancing mime entitled *Kuklite* (puppets), was an encore performance that I had done in Sofia, Bulgaria, choreographed by a man named Elija of the Pirin State Ensemble. After that performance, Bulgarian children had run on stage with bouquets of roses for me chanting, Kukla! Kukla! (little puppet girl). Both performances, Heinz Hall and the Bulgarian performance, were quite memorable dance experiences for me.

Graduation was set for a balmy day in May, but I didn't attend the ceremony. My diploma, so coveted, arrived rather unceremoniously in the mail. Instead, we boarded the bus for our Western tour. This tour had special meaning for me since two of the stops would be Los Angeles where my stepfather's sister and her family lived, and San Francisco where my mother's brother, Wallace—that member of the once devilish duo, lived. Since the death of his parents in 1959 and then in 1961, Wallace, deathly afraid of flying, never returned East. Wallace was my favorite uncle, and I couldn't wait to see him. But that didn't happen. We were into our third week of Western Tour performing in the highly technological community of Los Alamos, New Mexico. For the past two months, I had noticed that my knee and leg kept collapsing. Several times during a performance, one of my male dance partners caught me before my leg went under. On reflection, I should have had it checked out. But in four years I had never missed a performance. Our bus driver and beloved friend, nicknamed Koc, joked, "Strong like bull, these Balkan women!" But I wasn't so strong. After a particularly grueling performance, we arrived at a reception hall. During these receptions, Tammies were expected to dance and mingle with the individuals responsible for booking the concert. I loved dancing and I loved mingling with people so this was never a chore for me. These receptions provided a winding down time after the exhausting two hour performance. I was dressed in a cute green and white summer dress with white, heeled sandals, with the backs of my heels exposed. Most dancers know that open heeled shoes are never safe. The risk of turning an ankle or foot is too great. I should have known better. In the middle of the dance, I felt and literally heard, a tremendous pop in my knee. My leg buckled, and one of the musicians, Steve Zegar, a dear friend to both Steve Vesolich and me, noticed my look of pain, ran over to the dance floor, picked me up, and carried me off like a little baby wrapped in a bundle.

The next day, the leg would not straighten at the knee. I hobbled along on one foot and tiptoed on the other. As long as the knee was bent, there was no pain. The male staff members lacked compassion. With their mentality of "the show must go on," they told me to flex it a little bit in the pool by swimming. One staff member said, "Aw, you'll be OK, just swim it off a little bit!" But swimming didn't help. They took me to the local hospital where the treatment unnerved me: Since the troupe was moving on to San Francisco, the doctors wanted to put me in traction. I started crying. To be alone in Los Alamos, New Mexico, with my leg in traction didn't appeal to me. I was crushed that I wouldn't be able to see my uncle, but I was more concerned about my leg. One of the female staff members, Pat French, took charge, and in true motherly fashion said, "You people put this girl on a plane, and send her home to her mother where she can get good care. This tour is just a month's tour, but her leg has to last her all her life. Besides, she's getting married!" Yes, and besides, I was getting married.

Chapter 27...Getting Married

Today I married my friend

Before departing for Western Tour, a blessing and then a crisis occurred in my romantic status. The spring of my senior year, Steve proposed to me. It happened at one of our favorite restaurants. After dinner, he placed that special black box in my hand, the one that causes every young woman in love to hold her breath as she gently opens the contents to reveal that most coveted stone: the engagement diamond. Had I gone to the jewelers to select the ring myself, which I had not, I would have chosen the exact diamond and setting. The proposal was not a surprise; we had been waiting for this time for four years. The next step was to talk to my parents. We called them and told them that we would be visiting them that weekend. When Steve asked them for permission, my mother seemed stunned. Even after our four years of dating, she seemed shocked that we actually were getting married. I was confused by her response:

"We thought that you would be coming back home after college to live here for awhile," she said. While my mother made no overtly warm response to us, she certainly had great plans for this news. As I mentioned before, Tammies, by contract, were not allowed to become engaged or married while in the ensemble. I still had another semester to complete, so we had agreed to keep this engagement a secret, telling no one but our parents. Certainly you could trust your own parents to keep a secret. But one of the parents, my mother, had a radio station with a vast listening audience in the ethnic community. For whatever reason, she decided to announce our engagement over the air. Of course, the directors and just about everyone else heard the news. Steve and I were quite upset, anticipating some disciplinary action from the directors, at least with regard to my performance contract. They, for some reason, chose not to comment or deal with the engagement. I went on Western Tour, severely tour the cartilage in my knee, prepared for knee surgery—and a wedding!

The wedding was set for October, since I loved autumn, plus this gave me time for recovery from my knee operation, scheduled for June. Before my operation, however, we made a cross country drive in the Open Road van back to the West, this time to Las Vegas, Nevada, so I could be a bridesmaid, crutches and all, in the wedding of my beloved Cousin Annette. Even though Annette's wedding would take place in the "Love Chapel" ala Vegas style, her Macedonian relatives would see to it that it would have an ethnic flavor to it, music, food, and dancing. Right after the wedding, I was wheeled on to the plane and sent back home for my scheduled knee surgery. In 1973, knee surgery was rather complex since this was way before arthroscopic knee surgery. Even though I was almost twenty-two, this was my first surgery and I was scared, especially with my mother three thousand miles away. Supporting me as best as they could were my father, my paternal grandmother Baba George, and of course, Steve. He was always there for me.

All of my life I have been dramatic, and I have obviously watched too many movies. Consequently, throughout the night on the eve of my surgery, I had these strange thoughts, "What if they do the wrong leg? What if they cut off my leg?" I kept looking down at my now unmarred leg, albeit bent with torn cartilage, and thought, "It'll never be the same." My roommate in the hospital, an elderly lady, didn't offer any words of comfort to me. When I voiced my fears, she responded with, "Oh, yeah. My sister had so much trouble with her leg after surgery. You'll see." But the strangest thing happened. My surgery scheduled for that June morning didn't take place for another month. As they wheeled me down to the operating room on a gurney, in my mildly sedated condition I overheard the doctor say, "This young woman can't have knee surgery. She cannot risk the anesthesia. Her blood count is too low."

It was low enough to give the doctors cause to believe that I had leukemia. But I didn't. After several spinal taps and blood tests, it was determined that I suffered from anemia, a type that people of Mediterranean descent often exhibited. The demanding schedule of the Tammies hadn't helped the situation. My all-expenses paid education at Duquesne did, indeed, have a price: torn cartilage and anemia. It took a month of special dieting, medicines, and resting to revive my blood count to a decent level. I had my surgery (without my leg—right or left—being cut off), went to rehab, and threw away my crutches just in time to get married.

The wedding, of course, could not occur without a few minor and a few major glitches. The first conflict was religion. Culturally, Steve and I had grown up similarly. His dad, fondly called Zuti (yellow) for his blonde hair as a boy, had an incredible voice and played on weekends in a tamburitzan band, just like my mother and grandfather. Steve's older brother Tom was a skilled musician and tamburitzan vocalist. The three Vesolich men had incredible talent. Their Slavic background was Croatian. Although Croatians speak the same language as Serbians and relatively a close language to the Macedonians, Croatians differ in one significant way: religion. While Serbians and Macedonians are staunch Eastern Orthodox Christians, Croatians are Roman Catholic. Many wars have been fought in the Old Country over this difference. Steve and I were both devout in our own particular faiths, so we had to resolve the choice of church for the ceremony. I felt strongly that it was traditionally the bride's choice for the ceremony. Besides, I was still an active member in the Holy

Trinity Orthodox Church, the very church where my roots ran deep. This church represented the final sacramental rites of my deceased loved ones: my father, Uncle Bobby, and Baba and Dedo Moisoff. I couldn't tear myself away from this place. We met with the Orthodox priest, a family friend, who told us that we would need to sign papers agreeing that our children would be baptized and raised Eastern Orthodox. We signed the papers. Attempting to be fair, I agreed to at least meet with the Roman Catholic priest. This was a new priest, not the priest from Steve's boyhood days. He, likewise, told us that we had to sign papers agreeing that our children would be baptized Catholic. As he handed us his papers to sign, he looked intently at me and questioned, "Why do you want to get married in that old Orthodox church, huh? We are modern. We have air conditioning here. And besides, those Orthodox women wear babushkas."

Unwittingly, that priest had sealed the decision for us to get married in the Orthodox church. He had insulted me, and Steve never tolerated anyone insulting me no matter who they were!

With that conflict resolved, we focused on the reception. We both decided that we wanted a traditional wedding, small, but traditional. But we hadn't reckoned with Mom's plans. Once Mom reconciled herself to the fact that I wasn't returning home to live, and that Steve and I would definitely get married, she threw herself into the planning of the wedding with incredible energy. Even though Steve and I voiced a preference for a small wedding, Mom had grand plans, and her plans prevailed. It was out of our control.

First, the wedding banns were read in church for three weeks. I always liked this tradition. If anyone had anything to say negatively about the wedding, now was the time. It also seemed to seal the agreement. If you had any doubts, three weeks of public announcements in front of a congregation that you knew since your toddler stage seemed to vaporize those doubts. It was a done deal. The priest, with his heavy European accent, also encouraged everyone to come to the wedding to support the couple, just as they had agreed to support me since early baptismal days. Mom was not to be outdone by the priest. She greatly increased the number of wedding guests by announcing the wedding, once again, over the air, via radio. Whether she was nervous that enough people would attend, we don't know. But she invited her radio audience to the wedding. In her mind, her radio audience comprised her friends, and that was probably true enough.

The Duquesne University Tamburitzans sent their bus filled with ensemble members, including three orchestras, to the wedding for both enjoyment as well as musical purposes. Their musical talents for us, their friends, was free of charge. The reception hall, the Mahoning Valley Country Club, gave the official count of guests at 1500 people. I'm not sure how accurate that count was; I just know that the banquet hall was packed with wedding guests. The guests represented people from all walks of life somehow connected with me, my mother, or Steve:

the mayor, church people, tamburitzans, school friends, five sets of family members, friends, the ethnic community, and finally, such diverse individuals that went by the names of Diamond Lil and Toothless John—immensely delighted to be invited to this wedding (thanks to the radio invitation).

The wedding celebration started at my house where a live tamburitzan orchestra, the Balkan Serenaders, came to *prati,* or serenade the bride to the church. I never touched hands with anyone before I got into the car. The *Stari Svat,* or old man of the wedding, my godfather, *Kum* George Raseta, came with a hanky and I grabbed the end of it as we literally danced to the car. The whole event was reminiscent of my own mother and father's wedding back in 1950.

My stepfather proudly walked me down the aisle. That was the last *Americanized* part of the ceremony. The rest of the ceremony was done in the Slavonic language with the traditional ceremony including the Dance of Isaiah. Here we had a few tense moments. During the dance of Isaiah, crowns are placed on the heads of the bride and groom as they move in a circle in the middle of the church. Kum George got confused and placed the large crown on my head and the small crown on Steve's head. But the *a cappella* music of the choir in four part harmony, with a solo by Mrs. Olga Tatalovich, was heavenly, so no one noticed, except my nervous sister-in-law, Bev Vesolich, who held her breath until the Dance of Isaiah was over. When the religious ceremony was completed, the wedding guests exited and literally there was dancing in the street in front of the Holy Trinity Orthodox Church.

The dancing continued at the reception to the sound of three live bands: two tamburitzan bands and one band for easy listening and dancing. We, the bride and groom, dutifully stayed in the reception line until 9:00 P.M. that evening, then we decided that was enough. The wedding had started at 3:00 P.M. that afternoon. To the protests of our photographer, we left the reception line, even though guests were still arriving, and the two of us danced and danced. To conclude the evening, Steve sang to me, and then we both sang a song to each other first in Slavic, and then translated the words into English:

Fala (Thank you):

Za vsaku dobru rec (For each and every good word)
Kaj reci si mi znala (That you once spoke to me dear)
Za vsaki pogled tvoj (For every loving glance)
Za vsaki smeh tvoj fala (For every smile, I thank you)
A ti si srce mi   (And in my heart remains)
Tak puno sunca dala (A love that lives forever)
Kaj morem ti neg rec (What more is there to say)
Od sega srca fala   (With all my heart, I now thank you)

Chapter 28...Teaching School

Reading and writing and 'rithmetic!

In the first months of our marriage, we followed a similar routine. During the week, we both taught in the public school system, Steve in social studies and I, English, speech, and journalism. At 3:00 P.M. each Friday when the school week ended, we both packed a little bag, hopped in separate cars, and joined our bands for various musical engagements. I continued to play music with my mother and the girls in our orchestra, "Libby's All Girl Tamburitzans." Steve, his father, his brother Tom, and two other musicians performed as the Vesolich Orchestra, later called *Cigani*. The hours were long, but the money was good. In addition, we joined forces as director and choreographer and worked with two performing ensembles of teenagers and children in the Beaver County area. Frequently, our ensembles received invitations to perform in different states as the guest ensembles. But the biggest goal of the year, the spring concerts which consisted of instrumentation, vocals, and choreography, always met with success. To make life even more hectic, Steve worked on a master's degree in guidance at Duquesne University, and I began working on a master's degree in education at Pennsylvania State University. We were young and had just the right amount of energy to maintain this hectic pace. Almost. The pace, combined with my proneness to anemia and a lousy immune system, took its toll. I found myself taking more sick days at school. One of these sick days proved to be disastrous. When I began my teaching career in the public school system, I landed a job in January, midterm, in a school district known for students with high disciplinary needs. A male teacher had decided that the job was too demanding, and he quit—right in the middle of the school year. As Providence would have it, on January 7, I dined with a Serbian Orthodox family in celebration of Orthodox Christmas. One of the guests that I met that evening was the principal of this school. He needed a teacher—immediately, and since I desperately needed a teaching job, it was a done deal.

I was twenty-two, only four years older than most of my students, in some cases, even less. They were feisty, but so was I. It was a good match. On my first day of school, I was instructed to walk through the boiler room to enter the building. It was a gloomy, dismal place and my mind raced to all the horrible teaching movies that I had ever seen. Entering my room on the first floor, packed with students, I paused for a breath. Immediately a tall, lanky boy stood up and challenged me in front of the class, "Lady, you ain't gonna last the day!" He grinned.

The second day, he issued a second challenge, "Lady, you ain't gonna last the week." Near the end of the week, another boy, this one not so lanky, stood up and taunted, "You so little and short, and we so tall, how you gonna teach us?"

"Well, you sit, and I'll stand, and no one will ever know the difference," I retorted. The class liked that. They howled. He sat. It was a good beginning. I knew that I had survived when at the end of the second week, one of the senior boys handed me a cigar in honor of his girlfriend who had just given birth to twins! The new teacher on the block received an education. To be sure, the semester continued with typical antics so adeptly demon- strated by students, but I learned two tips about teaching: First, always keep a sense of humor. Secondly, see the worth of each student. I started to look beyond the classroom, and my eyes were opened to the enormous talents of these teenagers, talents in athletics, music, poetry.

Never one to hide my emotions, I visibly showed that I was impressed. They liked that. But I had miles to go before I tamed this group of students. One week, I was out with bronchitis. When I came back to school, walking through the boiler room, a colleague met me and said, "Oh, boy, what an ugly mess, eh?"

"What are you talking about?" I asked.

"Your room, of course. Wow, did they trash it!"

I started to laugh, "Ha! You really had me going

there, for a minute."

"No, no, I'm not joking around. When you were out, they had a male substitute teacher, an elderly guy. While he was in the room, they trashed the room, ripping posters, breaking his glasses, dumping garbage, knocking books off the shelves. It's a real mess. They notified the police. There's big trouble here." I couldn't believe it. The other thing that I couldn't believe was why they hadn't cleaned the room which still was in a state of disorder. Yes, my colleague was correct: they certainly had trashed the room. I went to the vice principal's office and for some reason I kept apologizing, "I'm so sorry this happened. I don't know what to say."

Overhearing this conversation, the guidance counselor, a no-nonsense woman loudly interjected, "What on earth are you apologizing for? It just shows us that when you are here, that group of hooligans in your classroom that we graciously call students—well, they are at least somewhat under control!"

"Yeaa!" I thought. Shoulders back, chin up, I went back to my classroom where thirty guilt-ridden faces greeted me. The chief offenders, now suspended, were not in the room, but these thirty students looked sheepish. It had finally dawned on them that in trashing the room, they had not punished the substitute teacher, but in reality, they had destroyed my stuff—stuff that had made their room a nicer place. Quietly, the class began cleaning the room. Some students offered copies of their poetry to mount on the walls, others sketched

English related drawings. I bought more borders and more posters, so essential in adding color to the drab setting of pea green walls, chipped beige tiles, and dusty blackboards. The room was back in shape. Things settled down and for the remainder of that school year, that elusive classroom goal occurred: learning! As I taught them grammar and composition, I shared tales of my Grandmother Annastasia's complexities with the English language. As they struggled with conjugating verbs, they appreciated hearing my grandmother's favorite expression, "How did you came, did you drove?" Again and again they would beg me to tell them stories about my grandmother. One student thought that it was quite ironic that my grandmother couldn't speak English very well, and here I was, their English teacher. That situation somehow offered hope to many of them.

Chapter 29...Raising a Family

Ne plac mala (Don't cry, little one)

After five years of marriage, I was going to have a baby. We were thrilled, the *we* being everyone in the family from grandparents to great-grandparents to cousins, aunts, brother, sister, uncles, etc. I continued to play music with the band and I taught school into the eighth month of my pregnancy. The teenage girls at my high school that were already mothers sat around me during lunch or study hall and offered tips on childbirth, establishing in a rather bizarre way, a bond between them and me. Some of the girls even visited the hospital the evening that I went into labor.

Throughout my pregnancy, I was high strung and over-concerned with every detail to the point of being illogical. My pregnancy jitters got a little out of hand during a routine exam when I was nearly seven months pregnant. My obstetrician was a fatherly type, but quite humorless, for the most part.

Delivering babies was his job, and that he did quite successfully for nearly thirty years. Feeling my tummy, this competent doctor said, "Hmm. I can't be sure. I'd have to do a sonogram, but I'm feeling two. Yep, I think—wait—yep there's one here. I think I feel the head here and maybe another one over here. I think that there might be two. Yep!"

Of course, the doctor was speculating that I might be having twins. But my mind, bordering on hysteria, went to a different place. I sprang from the table, examination gown falling and exclaimed, "Doctor, do you mean to tell me that my baby is going to have one body and two heads?" This no-nonsense doctor sat down on his stool, and after a very long pause, did something that I had never seen him do before; he laughed. Not just a little chuckle, but a full blown belly laugh as he exclaimed, "No, Ma'am, when they have two bodies, they usually have two heads! Heh! Heh! I was thinking that maybe you are having twins!"

I lay back on the table, discreetly rearranged my fallen examination gown over the proper places and with as much dignity as I could muster, simply said, "Oh. I see."

The sonogram revealed that it wasn't twins. The baby had been moving enough for the doctor to speculate about twins. Based on my ridiculous comment, I'm sure that he went home that night and had a good laugh with his wife concerning one of his crazy patients.

In addition to my lack of clear thinking, my aversion to germs and my standard for cleanliness during this pregnancy reached a level that would have pleased the staff in an operating room. At a baby shower thrown by my mother and her friends, I received the usual assortment of baby paraphernalia: baby clothes, furniture, blankets, etc. Several of the packages had been creatively decorated with baby rattles. When I took the large number of baby rattles home, I decided that they were unsanitary, so I pulled out the largest stock pot that I could find, filled it with water and Dreft detergent and boiled all the baby rattles. I wanted them clean. That they were, as well as melted together in one fine mess of pink, yellow, and blue plastic.

Finally, our baby daughter was born. We named her Stephanie Ann. The name Stephanie, which was Greek for crowned one, honored her father and grandfather. The Ann, the diminutive form of Annastasia, which was Greek for one who shall rise again, honored both me and her great-grandmother, Annastasia.

In true Slavic fashion, the whole family on both sides came to the maternity ward to await her arrival. My mother, whom we quickly named BabaLu (a combination of the Slavic word for grandmother and Lu for Ljubica), ran to the store and purchased Stephanie's first dress, pink with burgundy trim on the pockets.

One month after the baby's birth, the family celebrated with a baby christening which, after the baptismal service, included tamburitzan music—reminiscent of my birthday celebration some twenty-six years earlier. It took awhile before my jittery nature with this baby settled down.

Two and a half years later, finally feeling somewhat confident in my skill as a mother, I was ready to make a go of it again. Our second child, a boy whom we named Stephen Adam, was born. The family, now fondly referred to as the "clan," arrived in full force to witness this second miracle. As all the relatives cooed at Baby Stephen in the hospital bassinette, one of the elderly relatives gave little two and a half year old Stephanie a life saver. Of course, she swallowed it whole and began to choke. None of my Moisoff family members respond to any crisis with any degree of calmness; this situation was no exception. Family members started screaming and yelling! Nurses ran toward the choking toddler. Someone had the presence of mind to gently use the Heimlich maneuver on Stephanie. The life saver was dislodged and Stephanie was fine. The only consequences of the event were Stephanie's wailing and the rest of the relatives blaming each other for the crisis. This would not be the last crisis involving babies and family members.

By the time Stephanie was four and Stephen eighteen months, my mother wanted the children to visit with her by themselves. "You are always too bossy and too persnickety with them when you are here," she said. "Let them come to my house without you." I agreed.

We packed their bags and off they went to their BabaLu's house, forty minutes away. They hadn't been there for very long when Stephanie reached out to pet the family dog, usually a gentle animal. For some reason, the dog bit her. It wasn't a big bite, but my mother knew that I would be upset. She called her family doctor and nervously asked, "Doctor, my dog bit my grandchild, what should I do?"

The doctor, a grumpy man, responded in his typical curt manner: "Did your dog have his rabies shots? Yes? Well, then it's OK. Don't bother me with silly things. Pour peroxide over the wound. You ought to know that." He hung up the phone. My mother was relieved, but she could see that Stephanie was really frightened by the dog. Not wanting her to grow up afraid of dogs, Mom decided to take Stephanie to see her neighbor's dog, a friendly, little dog that everyone in the neighborhood loved. Stephanie, who was quite a gentle child and not rambunctious in any way, once again reached over to pet the dog. For some strange reason, maybe sensing her fear, the dog bit her. This was the second bite in one afternoon and Stephanie was hysterical; Stephen also cried on behalf of his sister. BabaLu made another phone call to the doctor. "OK, Doc. This is Libby again. Uh, well, I've got to tell you, the dog bit my grandchild."

"What? What's the matter with you people?" the doctor bellowed. "I told you that it was fine. Your dog had his shots, right? Your granddaughter is fine."

"No, Doc," my mother stammered as she spoke to this doctor who was also a family friend. "This time another dog bit her—the neighbor's dog."

"What? OK. This dog is a family pet—so it had its shots, right?" the doctor asked.

"Yea, I think so," was Mom's nervous reply.

"OK. Your granddaughter is fine. Gee whiz! Keep that child away from dogs, will you!" he roared.

Babalu brought both Stephanie and Stephen into her living room and isolated them from any animal. She sat on her chair and carefully watched the children as they played. She wasn't going to take any more chances, but for some unknown reason, Stephen leaned over and bit Stephanie on the leg. This bite had broken more skin than both dog bites combined! Mom's friend who had been at Babalu's house when all of this was happening added her thoughts, "You know, they say that the bite of a human being, because of the saliva, is worse than any animal's bite." So for the third time in one afternoon, Mom called the doctor.

"Doctor, this is Libby again."

"What is it now, Libby?"

"Well, uh, you see," she nervously stammered, "the kid bit my granddaughter and broke the skin." This doctor, never known for his kind, bedside manner bellowed, "What the heck are you doing with a kid in your house? Who keeps a goat in the house?" he asked.

"No, no! Not a goat! The kid, the kid is her brother! Her brother bit her!"

"You know what, Libby," he muttered almost in a monotone voice, "send that child back home to Pennsylvania with her mother." She did.

Chapter 30...
Developing Musicians

Do re me, do re me
The first three notes just happen to be
Do re me

As parents with a strong musical background, Steve and I were determined to encourage and develop any musical gifts that surfaced in our children. As early as age five, our daughter Stephanie began taking piano lessons. By the end of that year, her competency on that instrument enabled her to perform at the spring recital, one of the youngest performers. Her little feet, clad in her shiny, black Mary Janes could barely reach the piano pedals. She sat down on the piano bench, neatly adjusted her navy and white dotted Swiss dress with the big red bow in the center, and began to play, her little fingers flying across the keys to the musical tune of "Riding on A Donkey."

By the time she reached high school, her

instructor requested that we find another piano instructor since Stephanie had far exceeded anything that she, the teacher, could impart at this level. Her instructor had sheepishly told us that she wanted to make this suggestion for years, but never could bring herself to part with Stephanie as her student, but she recognized that she had to do what was best for Stephanie musically.

During her college years, Stephanie traveled worldwide as the accompanist of the Genevans, a forty-member choral ensemble from Geneva College in Beaver Falls, Pennsylvania. One of her most memorable performances with this ensemble was at the Royal Albert Hall in London. Because Stephanie was also a gifted singer and an excellent sight reader of music, her choral directors found her most competent in accompanying the ensemble.

Since Stephanie had been so successful in her piano studies, we led our son Stephen down the same path. He willingly sat through the lessons, but it was apparent that his heart was not in this instrument. An energetic boy, he needed to move around, and he definitely needed to take center stage. Stephanie and Stephen were very close as brother and sister, each one offering tremendous support of the other. But playing the piano, we could see, would only keep Stephen in the shadow of his sister, so we switched him to guitar so he would have the opportunity to soar on his own, and soar he did! By the time he reached his early twenties, he was on his way to a successful career as a musician and songwriter, winning acoustic guitar and songwriting competitions, making CD's, and performing all over the Pittsburgh area.

During their elementary, middle school, and high school years, both children competed and won lead roles in concerts and musicals including *Fiddler on the Roof, Brigadoon, Oliver!* and *Sound of Music.* By the time Stephen was in junior high, his school participated in the Henry Mancini Awards. The award ceremony, named in honor of Mr. Henry Mancini, who had grown up in Aliquippa, Pennsylvania, not more than ten miles from our home, was considered highly prestigious. To these high school students performing in a musical, these awards were every bit as important to them as an Oscar award might be to a Hollywood actor. Judges with professional backgrounds attended the various high school musicals in the county and tallied votes for the best of the lot. Stephen took home several trophies for Best Male Performer and Noteworthy Performance. His high school won the award for Best High School Musical so many times that other schools enviously accused his school, Beaver County Christian, of scouting and recruiting students for these musicals, just as a football or basketball coach recruits his athletes. Of course that wasn't true. While they studied piano, voice, and guitar, we enrolled the children in a local junior tamburitzan orchestra and dance ensemble. Like our musical experience so many years ago, these junior tamburitzan groups trained children and teens in the folk music and dancing of their Slavic heritage. We, their parents, had been asked to be the director and choreographer of these ensembles. Growing up loving this music, we assumed that our children, now third generation Americans, would feel the same; that they would want to follow in our footsteps and the footsteps of their grandparents and great-grandparents. As if history were repeating itself, our children would now experience the formidable task of reconciling their all-American life with their ethnic background just as we did. But these were different times. The ethnic community of our teen years had changed. After several years of lessons and numerous concerts, we could see that the children did not enjoy these musical endeavors. They preferred performing on their own, or with the family. But their experiences in the youth orchestras and folk dancing groups acquainted them with the language and they both learned how to dance the folk dances and how to sing the ethnic songs.

Each summer, we would join my mother and perform at an event called "Concert in the Park" to a very large and enthusiastic audience. Our family produced quite an eclectic sound mixing our tamburitzan instruments with Stephanie's electric piano and Stephen's guitar. We began our concert singing the old, Slavic traditional folk songs including my Grandmother Annastasia's favorite song, *Mladi Kapetane* (Young Captain)—that folk song lamenting a young woman's lover going to fight in the Balkans. Closing the concert, the family, in four-part harmony, sang Gospel and contemporary Christian songs. This was very special for us, personally, for by this time in our lives, we had begun to sing a new song.

Chapter 31...Singing A New Song

Sing joyfully to the Lord,
Sing to Him a new song.
Psalm 33

There is a verse in the Bible that reads, "You will seek me and find me when you seek me with all your heart. I will be found of you" (Jeremiah 29:13). As a young man, in his twenties, this became Steve's quest, and this spiritual quest changed both of our lives. First of all, he left his teaching career and entered seminary to become a pastor, thereby, changing life as we knew it. For us, the most wonderful thing had happened. But not all of our friends and relatives felt that way. One distant relative, obviously annoyed by what he called our "religious bent" grumbled, "Why did you go off and find religion? If you needed to do something different, why didn't you just go off and do drugs or drink, ya know, like normal people do?"

When I excitedly told one of my mother's best

friends what had happened to us, she sniffed and said, "I know what happened to you—you left the church."

Yes, we had left both the Orthodox and Roman Catholic churches and began attending a Protestant denomination. It wasn't that Steve couldn't find answers to his spiritual quest in the Catholic or Orthodox churches, for he could. Wherever the redeeming message of Christ is preached, the **truth** is there. In the Gospel of John, Jesus says, "I am the way and the **truth** and the life" (John 14: 6).

Steve, however, answered what some would refer to as "his calling" to enter the ministry. I, who had grown up worshiping in a liturgical church with candles, ornate icons, priests in resplendent robes, and incense burning altar boys, now sat in the stark sanctuary of a Protestant church.

As Steve intensely studied the scriptures and lived his life as faithfully and closely as he could to the message of the Bible, he challenged my commitment to God and my faith. For even though I had loved God all of my life, much of my belief system had been based on traditions and rituals—even fear.

One day during a very casual conversation, he asked me a question that was anything but casual, "Stace, if you were to die tonight, where would you spend eternity?" Thoughts raced in my head. What was he talking about? Was this a joke? I had grown up in the church. Where did he think that I would spend eternity? I was a Christian and a very good one, thank you very much! I opened my mouth to answer. I started to form the words "Heaven, of course." But I couldn't say it. How silly at that moment I thought of a line from the Shakespearean play, *Macbeth.* In the play the protagonist, Macbeth, has just murdered the good King Duncan. As he flees from the scene of his hideous crime, he passes by the sleeping quarters of the king's sons, heirs to the throne of Scotland. Pausing by their door, he hears them talking and saying their prayers, not realizing that their beloved father had been assassinated. And as they close their prayers, Macbeth wants to say "Amen," but he cannot. He, in an agitated state, asks his wife the villainous Lady Macbeth, "But wherefore could not I pronounce 'Amen'? I had most need of blessing, and 'Amen' stuck in my throat." Not to compare myself with the evil Macbeth, hopefully, but for a brief instant I could not answer or say heaven in response to Steve's question, and I had most need of saying that I would spend eternity in heaven. I stammered a weak response to Steve's question:

"Steve, I just don't know." In the most loving, gentle voice Steve leaned closer to me and said, "Stace, without the shedding of blood, there is no forgiveness of sin."

What had caused him to say that? I was astounded. All my life, I had loved the Lord, yet I wrestled with the logic of His crucifixion. I accepted it. I even worshiped Christ for doing this, but it made no sense to me. My thinking always concluded with, "Why would God demand such a brutal death for His Son? I didn't ask Him to do that! I wouldn't have killed anybody or anything like that!"

Steve continued to speak offering an analogy,

"You know, in the Old Testament, the Hebrew people brought two goats to the priest on the Day of Atonement, that day of reconciliation with God. Aaron, the priest, sacrificed the first goat, but he held the second goat in his arms, confessed the sins of the children of Israel on that goat, and then released it to flee into the wilderness. This second goat was called the scapegoat because it had all the sins of Israel thrust upon it, but it had escaped death, while the other innocent goat had been sacrificed for the atonement of sins. Jesus is that innocent goat, actually the Lamb of God. You and I, we are like that scapegoat, so full of sin, but given the opportunity to flee from our sins through the sacrifice of another." He reminded me that there was a parallel to this in the New Testament when both Jesus and Barabbas, under Pontius Pilate, were brought before the crowd. Barabbas, a convicted murderer whose name meant the son of a father was released according to the demands of the crowd, while Jesus the Son of the Father was brutally scourged and crucified.

In this explanation, Steve unknowingly had torn down a tremendous stumbling block in my faith. But I had to release more spiritual junk in my life. Since childhood, I held on to the belief that God was a God of wrath and revenge, ready to smite me if I did anything wrong. Most certainly, that thinking had formed in early childhood.

In the Orthodox Church, one prepared for Holy Communion by fasting for a week without eating meat or dairy products. Twelve hours before Holy Communion was taken, food and water were prohibited. If you broke this fast at any time before Communion, even if it were a few hours before the Communion was taken, you would have to start fasting from the beginning of the next week. Not only were special dietary laws called *posni* observed, the week preceding communion was a time of prayer, meditation, and serious confession. On the eve before receiving communion, you met face to face with the Orthodox priest to confess your sins. I couldn't have been more than eleven years old during one memorable confession. In the sanctuary, devoid of all lights except a few candles, the priest, dressed in somber black robes, approached me carrying a large painting. As he got closer, my eyes focused on that painting which depicted dozens of people in various stages of agony and torture all being consumed by hell's flames. In a stern voice, accented by his fingers tapping on that frightening painting, he asked, "Are you a good girl?" Concentrating solely on that macabre painting, I didn't immediately answer the priest. He asked again, "Are you a good girl because if you are not, do you see this picture?"

"Yessss," I gasped, eyes widened in terror as I focused on a particular individual in the painting who, obviously, suffered greatly.

"If you aren't a good girl, you will go to hell like the people in this painting!" he continued while tapping on the glass enclosure over the painting. I promptly started to confess anything that I could remember.

"Well, sometimes I sass my mother, and sometimes I am mean to my sister, and sometimes I lie, and then there was that one time that I..." Obviously pleased by my verbal purging, the priest uttered, "Good, good, good."

It wasn't that the priest was an evil man. He really wasn't. In fact, when I reflect back on his character, he actually was a great man of God who truly loved the Lord. But during confessionals, he used hell and brimstone tactics, and the fear that he wanted to accomplish certainly worked on me! Steve's conversation in which he reminded me that God was indeed just, but that He was a loving God, melted away much of that fear. The sacrificing of God's only Son wasn't an act of wrath, but the most extraordinary act of love.

At this point in my life, I was able to surrender all religious baggage and childhood fears. My relationship with Jesus Christ wasn't based on what I had done, but what the Savior had done! "This is love; not that we loved God, but that He loved us and sent His son as an atoning sacrifice for our sins" (1 John 4: 10). I uttered a simple and cleansing prayer, "Lord, I surrender my life to you. Do whatever you will with my life." I was free to give up everything and anything to serve Him. And I did.

Chapter 32...
Reconciling Old and New
Inlaid Pearl

*Tad moja dusa sretno slavi Te (Then sings my soul, my
    savior, God to thee)*
*Silni Boze, silni Boze!   (How great thou art, how great
    thou art!)*

For me, because of the intertwining of the Orthodox religion with the Slavic culture, I thought that if I gave up one, I would have to give up the other. The first thing that I gave up was my career as a professional musician, since so many of the jobs took place in cultural settings. Next, I quit my side job as a choreographer. Finally, I quit teaching in the public school system and began teaching in a private, Christian school. I wanted to create that image of the perfect pastor's wife. Somehow, in my mind, I couldn't see how my ethnic heritage could blend in this new walk of life. Some of our friends, especially those who had purchased records by Steve or by me asked, "Hey, we don't hear you guys anymore. Are you doing anything with music?" Steve had a ready answer, "We're singing for the Lord."

And, indeed, that's what we were doing, singing Gospel music, both in our own church where Steve served as pastor, and as vocalists invited to other churches for concerts. Steve also served as a guest speaker in many churches in the Pittsburgh area. We joined choirs, led musical productions, used our vocal talents on mission trips and other ministries, and even performed on the local Christian television station. As early as pre-school age, we incorporated the talents of our two children in our ministry of music. Sometimes we would use our tamburas to glorify God in music. To our amazement, the Christian community loved when we played these instruments to the tune of traditional hymns and choruses. Often, we would create musical arrangements that had an Israeli sound to them. The congregation loved these arrangements and would often clap in rhythm as we performed.

By now, I no longer played the tamburitzan instrument of my youth. On our second wedding anniversary Steve surprised me with the most incredible gift: a beautifully handcrafted new *prim*, that stringed instrument that I had played since age six. But this instrument was far superior to any other instrument in my extensive collection. Steve had traveled to Lawrenceville, Pennsylvania, where an eighty-year old, master tamburitzan craftsman, Mr. Nick Orehovich, lived. The two men met and discussed the design of the instrument. This prim would be a custom made design of cherry wood and an inlaid mother-of-pearl inset of the letter S for Stacie, surrounded by inlaid mother-of-pearl flowers. The design had special meaning, not just with the S for Stacie. The inlaid pearl matched the pearl on my grandfather's antique mandolin; the flowers represented my love of gardening. Meticulously crafted, this turned out to be the last instrument that Mr. Orehovich made before his death. It had the most resonating sound of any stringed instrument in my collection, or in several other collections of fellow musicians. Due to the expert craftsmanship, I never developed any calluses on my fingers. Mr. Orehovich had so masterfully crafted this instrument that I barely had to touch the frets to create a clear sound that could be heard above any other sound in the orchestra. This instrument truly was a work of art.

Could something so beautiful be unacceptable to God? In my attempt to be the perfect pastor's wife, I had suppressed a rich heritage that was a vital part of me. It was another family tragedy that caused me to balance my new walk of faith with the heritage of my birth.

On February 17, 1984, the family, jokingly called the clan, was getting ready for a big celebration, the third birthday of my son Stephen. We couldn't have just a little party for children; we had to have a big shindig for everyone! But the party never happened that day. Instead, as I was preparing a special meat dish for the party, I received a phone call from a nurse in the emergency room of the hospital. My father-in-law had suffered a massive heart attack. My husband rushed over to the hospital. It was too late.

Steve called me and in a most painful voice said, "The worst has happened." My wonderful father-in-law was dead, and he had died on his beloved grandson's birthday. We never had a chance to say goodbye. We were devastated. But it was through his death that we were reminded of a beautiful promise in the Bible, "God does not show favoritism, but accepts men from every nation who fear him and do what is right." (Acts 10:34)

In our attempt to walk a certain way in the faith, we had shunned anything that reminded us of our past. For many things, this was good, but not for all things. Steve's father, who clearly kept our ethnic traditions, was a man who "feared the Lord and did what was right." As we grieved for this wonderful man, it seemed as if the Lord was reminding us of this promise. So slowly, our lives changed again. They didn't go back to the way they were, thankfully, but instead became a meshing of who we were, and who God intended us to be.

Our church ministry was all-encompassing, yet we managed to blend our ethnic heritage, particularly the music, with our ministry. The Lord placed on our hearts a burning desire to tell the ethnic community, of whom we knew so well, that a relationship with Jesus Christ involved more than participating and keeping traditions and rituals. It involved the total surrendering of a life to the lordship of

Jesus Christ. It blessed my heart that the first people to receive this message of life were members of our own family, including my mother.

On a professional level, I continued to teach school in the private, Christian sector, which I loved, while I worked on various writing projects and endeavors with English teachers in the public school system, as well as working as a writing consultant for teachers taking education courses at the University of Pittsburgh. When I taught writing and grammar seminars, I shared stories of my grandmother and her struggles with English syntax as she would ask, "How did you came, did you drove?" And my students would chuckle and ask to hear more stories about my grandmother.

I resumed teaching folk dancing classes, only this time at a leisurely pace and only for high school and college classes. Whenever I taught music or dance lessons, I displayed my grandfather's antique mandolin with the inlaid mother-of-pearl butterfly, and then I would lay it side by side with my prim with the inlaid mother-of-pearl S for Stacie surrounded by the pearl flowers. I would tell them how special these instruments were to me, precious heirlooms that reflected four generations of family musicians. And many times I had the opportunity to tell them that as precious as these instruments were to me, I had something even more precious and more beautiful than those instruments with their inlaid pearl, and that was my faith in Jesus Christ.

Epilogue

Chapter 33...
Gathering of the Clan

Toje zivot moj (That's life)
Toje ljubav ot nas (That's love)

I always teased my mother about being elderly, but never living or acting her age. The family loved to visit a spectacular amusement park in Sandusky, Ohio, called Cedar Point, labeled the roller coaster capital of the world. Some of the hills on the various coasters such as the *Magnum XL* and the *Millennium Force* reached heights of 200 and 300 feet before dropping. Mom, now in her seventies, ran with her grandchildren to get a good spot in line to board the coasters. Yet, when we entered the park to purchase our tickets, she proudly displayed her "Ohio Buckeye Card" which granted her a senior citizen's discount. I teased her, "Mom, you big phony! Those

Buckeye Cards are for typical senior citizens who waddle up and down the midway licking vanilla ice cream cones. Not one of them will be in line for the *Magnum XL-200*—only you. She grinned impishly and as she ran in line shouted, "Come on, Stace! Let's try to get the front seat of the coaster!"

Even in her seventies, pushing the rules to the limit and moving at fast speeds seemed to be synonymous with her character. It was great for her, and definitely kept her young, and reciprocally, her energy swept us along with her.

On one family vacation, we decided to rent wave runners at a lovely inlet at Hilton Head Island, South Carolina. The rental cost was a bit high, so we compromised by having two riders per wave runner. After everyone paired off, Mom was assigned to me. Reluctantly, she agreed to ride with me. "OK," she acquiesced, "I'll ride with you, but I have to drive." The young attendant, a little concerned over this grandmother driving one of his wave runners, came over to give us our mandatory instructions: "Ma'am, y'all will want to hold on firmly to the handlebars, and let me just show you, a minute here, how to operate this machine." His Southern hospitality was just a bit too slow for Mom. Ignoring him, she slammed her foot on the accelerator and dashed off into the ocean as I scrambled to adjust my legs on the sides of the wave runner. I looked over my right shoulder and noticed dolphins playfully jumping in the waves, keeping pace with us. As I held her tightly around the waist I yelled, "Slow down! Slow down!" She ignored me. We hit the oncoming waves at full throttle! When we docked the wave runners at the end of our allotted time (which surprised me that she had actually abided by the rules), she indignantly looked at me and then pouting she informed one of my teenage children:

"I'm never riding with your mother again. She wants to go too slow." The young attendant at the dock was stunned, "Wow! You all could have fooled me on this one! I never thought that she would even get on one of these let alone go that fast. Hmm! Hmm! That's some grandma you kids have there!" Yes, she was.

And now that grandma was turning seventy-five, and we made plans for a very special party. My cousin Nettie reminded me that when her own mother, my Tete Annette, had turned seventy-five, her two sisters had flown to Las Vegas where she lived to celebrate with her. Now both Annette and Stella, my mom's two older sisters were gone, so were all of her brothers, including her beloved younger brother Wallace. She was the only living child of Annastasia and Dimko Moisoff, but the second and third, and even the fourth generation of Moisoff relatives wanted to celebrate the remarkable life of Libby. Since she had musical engagements every weekend, the synchronizing of this celebration would take some doing. At age seventy-five, my mother's calendar and daily planner looked like it belonged to a business executive. We set the bait: her grandchildren wanted to honor her with a special dinner at a posh Pittsburgh restaurant. Since their Babalu, my mother, could never say no to them, we knew that she would clear her calendar -so we thought. We sent invitations to the family members and also her closest friends. Due to the enormous number of friends and acquaintances that my mother had, we had to limit the invitations to those individuals that had a very special connection with my mother's life. One of her special friends designed and ordered T shirts with a photo of Libby on them. Written in boldface were the words, "Libby the Tamburitzan Sweetheart." All party guests were encouraged to wear their T shirts to the celebration. I hired a caterer for the dinner that would be held in the fellowship hall of our church. As I busied myself with the task of creating party favors and centerpieces, all with the color red, her favorite color, I received a disturbing phone call one week before the party. It was my mother's very close friend Linda.

"Stacie, are you aware that your mother is playing music on the date of her birthday party." This information came after the invitations and the confirmations to those invitations had been received. Relatives from all over the country would be arriving in Pittsburgh in a few days. My plans had been grand, and now the party girl herself was thwarting them. I started to panic.

"Linda, I can't believe this! How could she do this to me!! I have to hang up right now and call my mother!" I immediately called her and in a voice that I used for a disobedient student I admonished, "What do you mean you are not coming to the dinner! What can you possibly be thinking?"

Mom, detecting the firmness in my voice paused

a beat, but then met the challenge, "What's the big deal? You know it's close to the Christmas season, and I always have to play at these annual Christmas parties." To make the situation even more pathetic, she went on to tell me that this particular Christmas party was the annual party for the Mentally Handicapped Children of Mahoning County. How could I deny these special needs children their music at their party? They loved my mother. "You know, we could celebrate another day. We don't have to have dinner RIGHT on that date," she suggested.

This was terrible. I had to think of something quickly. I was desperate. So I concocted a little, or maybe not so little, lie. "Mom! You *have* to go to dinner with us on that day. The kids have been planning and saving for months for this particular day. It took a lot of effort to get this reservation at this really wonderful Pittsburgh restaurant. It's on Mt. Washington overlooking the city of Pittsburgh (Mom loved Mt. Washington), and you know how hard it is to get a reservation! We've arranged for special seating by the window overlooking the entire city and the Ohio River. You know how wonderful that is. By this point, I was desperate. She didn't budge. I became more emphatic, "I will be so upset with you," and then I tagged on the clincher, "And I will never talk to you again if you disappoint your grandchildren and don't come to the restaurant that day!"

Though she recognized that threat as high drama, she acquiesced. I sighed with relief as I heard her say, "OK. OK. I'll cancel my job and I'll call the program director at the home for these handicapped children. She'll just have to reschedule me on another date." My heart had a little stab of pain and a large stab of guilt as I thought of those poor children, but I couldn't do anything about it. My only consolation was that she would reschedule the date for them.

The day of the big 75th birthday party arrived with Mom still believing that she was on her way to a dinner with her children and grandchildren at the Georgetowne Inn Restaurant on Mount Washington in Pittsburgh, Pennsylvania. All the guests were tucked into their hiding places in the church fellowship hall ready to yell "Surprise!" Mom, who was about thirty minutes late by now, phoned me from her cell phone. "Hi, Stace. I know that I am late, but I am almost at your house."

"Where <u>exactly</u> are you?" I asked.

"Chippewa." Now the township of Chippewa is approximately a half hour from my mother's home and about twenty-five minutes from mine, so it often served as our halfway meeting point. But whenever my mother was on her way to my house, she would always tell me that she was in Chippewa, no matter where she precisely was. She could be two miles from her own driveway and she would say Chippewa. It got to be a joke for us. No matter where you were, you said Chippewa. So I asked her again,

"No, Mom, really, where are you?"

"Chippewa! I'll be there soon."

Normally, I would be upset with her for being late. This should have been a clue to her, but I just cooed, "OK, when you get here, that will be fine, but don't go to my house. Stop at the church. We are all there."

"What are you doing there?" she inquired. I had already prepared an explanation for the numerous cars in the parking lot just in case she became suspicious.

"Well, you know that nice girl from our church—Alissa? Well, she and her husband Ben are moving to Toledo, and the church is having a dinner for her. We just have to make an appearance and then we'll leave. OK?" (That part was true. Alissa and Ben were moving, but, of course, we were not having a dinner for them that afternoon.)

"Oh, Ok. Maybe I should give her some money as a gift," Mom said.

"No, no. You don't have to. We'll just go down-stairs for a few minutes to make an appearance, and then we will leave."

Mom arrived a few minutes later and I met her at the door. She was dressed in a lovely red and white sweater. Perfect! Her outfit went wonderfully with the decor.

"Hi, Mom." I gave her an affectionate birthday kiss. "OK, let's go downstairs to make our appear-ance." As we approached the fellowship hall, she joked and said, "Boy, it sure smells good in here. Maybe we shouldn't go out to eat, but eat here instead."

She opened the door to a thunderous round of HAPPY BIRTHDAY! She was stunned as she took in the sights of best friends and family members that she hadn't seen for over a year. She wept with joy, but the best was yet to come. After dinner we asked everyone to go upstairs to participate in an interactive theatrical production of "The Life of Libby." And then the stories began, those same stories that had been told for years and years. Only this time, rather than sharing family tales around the dinner table, we dramatized. Sandy, head covered with the Slavic woman's *babuska*, portrayed our beloved Baba Annastasia Moisoff, while my husband Steve portrayed Grandfather Dimko, accents of both grandparents included. I had fun reenacting the part of my mother as a disobedient child stamping her feet when she couldn't have her way. Josh, my son-in-law, portrayed the other part of that devilish duo, Uncle Wallace. As the play progressed, Cousin Vicki portrayed the part of the nurse at the hospital calling me "My Little Georgie Porgie." Stephanie, my daughter, portrayed me as a child. To encourage audience participation and response, Cousin Annette "Nettie" held large cue cards for the audience. Everyone had a part in the play, just as everyone in that room had some connection with the actual memories of my mother's life. Here we all were, reenacting my grandmother using *Americanski* psychology on her Ljuba, and that little Ljuba jumping in corn stalks. We laughed as we created the scene of Baba Moisoff huffing and puffing from exhaustion as Mom tried to pick her up at McKelvy's department store. And we imitated Annastasia innocently asking, "How did you came? Did you drove?" The finale of the program was music, of course, as we blended our tamburitzan instruments with the piano and guitar accompaniment of my son Stephen and daughter Stephanie, joined by son-in-law Josh Wilsey. After singing some Slavic songs, the last selection, sung both in English and Slavic was "You've Got To Give A Little" The last line of that song goes, "That's the story of, that's the glory of love." And in that room so full of music, there was love. I sat back and took it all in, giving thanks to the Lord that I was a part of this rich heritage, and that so many decades ago, a young woman named Annastasia and her husband Dimko left that Macedonian village bound for a better life for their posterity. And through the incredible grace of God, here we were.

We shared the legacy of the music, the love— the faith. In our hands, we held a tangible memento of that heritage moving on to the fourth and fifth generation of Moisoff family members— the mandolin with inlaid pearl. I hummed to myself, "That's the story of, that's the glory of love."

Resources

Anthropology of East Europe. (1993). *War among the Yugoslavs*, Vol II.

Council for Immigrant Research. (1894-1924). Philadelphia, Pennsylvania.

Chupovski, D. (1913). Macedonia and the Macedonians. *Makedonski Golos*.

Documents of the Continued Existence of Macedonia and the Macedonian Nation for Over 2,500 Years. (2001).

Drumm, D & Drumm, P. (2003). Interview. Circleville, West Virginia.

Duff, O. (2004). Project Advisor. Oakland: University of Pittsburgh.

Fill, L. Personal diaries (1941-1963). Campbell, Ohio.

Galida, F. (1976). *Fascinating history of the city of Campbell*. State College, PA: Jostens.

Gourley, C. (2002). *A nation of immigrants*. New Jersey: Writing! Publishers.

Heimreich, E.C. (2003). *The diplomacy of the*

Balkan Wars, 1912-1913. Columbia University Press.

History of Macedonia. (2001). *The Balkan Wars and the partition of Macedonia*. Macedonian newspapers and archives.

Holcomb, B. (2003). Interview. Conway, South Carolina.

Kerner, R. (Ed). (1949). *Yugoslavia*. Los Angeles: University of California Press.

Lesko, A. (2000). Interview. Las Vegas, Nevada.

Macedonian Academy of Sciences and Arts. (2001). Council for research into South-Eastern Europe. *History of Macedonia*.

Ohio Historical Center. (2004) Columbus, Ohio.

Patrone, I. (2000). Interview. Youngstown, Ohio.

Moisoff, A. & Moisoff, D. (1912-1961). Collaborated accounts of the Moisoff family history. Information provided by the family of Dimko and Annastasia Moisoff.

Moisova, S. (1999). Collaborated accounts of the Moisova family history. Information provided by the family of Spasia Moisova, sister of Dimko Moisoff.

Shopov, S & Damjanovki, C. (1995). *Images of Bitola and Prilep, Macedonia*. Grolier.

The Quest Study Bible. (1994). *New International Version*. The Zondervan Corporation.

Young, G. (2003). *Nationalism and the war in the Near East*. Columbia University Press.

Youngstown Historical Center of Industry and Labor. (1916-1980). Archives Library. Youngstown, Ohio.

Youngstown Sheet & Tube Company Report. (1950). *Fifty Years in Steel.*

Printed in the United States
40482LVS00001B/23